DEDICATION

Cara was going to write a dedication, but she missed the deadline because she was out chasing the Northern Lights.

CHAPTER 1

Holy fuck, I'm gonna die.

Quinn screwed his eyes shut and gripped the armrests so hard that his knuckles turned white. He wasn't all that well-traveled, but this couldn't be normal. This much turbulence had to mean he was about to plummet to a certain death.

So why the hell was the pilot laughing at him?

The small plane jerked and made sure Quinn's heart stayed in his throat. Every fall caused him to consider becoming religious, and with every bump he came up with a new inscription for his gravestone.

"Here lies the splattered remains of a guy who never should've ventured up to Alaska."

"Don't forget to breathe!" The pilot laughed, his gruff voice almost drowned out by the roar of the engine. Or was it the blizzard?

Did it fucking matter?

When he turned twenty-five last month, he should've thought about the fact that it would be his last birthday. If he'd known, he would've…maybe gone out to get laid or something. Instead, he'd been busy planning the scheme of his life with his best friend.

Logan was a few years older, and last week was the second time he'd shipped off to work construction in the Middle East. But not before helping Quinn land his own gig in construction. Or maybe construction was a stretch. The ad had been for a handyman, and Quinn wanted this particular job.

It had taken him weeks to convince Logan to help him, and after much begging and bribing, Logan had pretended to be Quinn during the phone interview.

"Okay, hold on! We're going down, kid!" the pilot announced.

"I fucking knew it." Quinn panicked.

The pilot snorted. "Not like that. We're *landing*, genius."

We'll see, Quinn thought miserably.

He was by no means some weak pussy. He could stand his own at six feet, and when he couldn't afford a gym membership, he went running on the beach. But what good would that do in the Alaskan wilderness? Born and raised on the Gulf Coast of Florida, he hadn't even owned a coat until he'd bought one for this trip. This was the first time he'd seen snow, and it was currently swirling around the tiny plane with the harsh winds.

At practically zero visibility, Quinn didn't see land until it was rushing up toward them as they approached the airstrip. He sucked in a breath and cursed himself for having opened his damn eyes in the first place. Then it got bumpier, though he allowed himself a small sigh of relief because they had officially touched ground.

He squinted out the window. The blizzard and the darkness made it impossible to see anything other than low hilltops and a rocky landscape covered in snow. He definitely didn't see the resort that was supposed to be *right there*.

A dream come true for the adventure-seeking explorer. In the main house, guests could live in bed-and-breakfast style. In the building to its left was a dormitory with bunk beds for backpackers. The staff lived in the building to the right. Close to hiking trails, wildlife, rock climbing, and fishing. There was a spa on the grounds, they had their own airstrip, a couple boats, an indoor pool, and Nome, the nearest city, was an hour *south* from here. By plane.

Before this, the farthest up north Quinn had traveled was

NORTHBOUND

Philadelphia.

His natural Florida tan wanted to take a hike at the mere mention of Alaska.

Now he was here, though. He'd traveled thousands of miles and spent every penny he owned to come to this very spot. And it wasn't for the resort he'd seen in the brochures. It wasn't to spend the next three months making eleven newly constructed cabins livable for the richer guests they'd cater to when spring came along.

He was here because he had questions for Declan, the man who'd dated Quinn's aunt six years ago.

*

One cabin down, ten to go. Declan sat down on the couch in his new home. After having lived in the staff house the past six years, he finally felt like he could relax.

Patrick and Nina, his brother and his sister-in-law, owned the O'Connor Adventure Retreat, and Declan was the man who made sure the place looked good. A cabin for himself had been his stipulation when he took the job. He'd known it was gonna be a while before they had enough money to expand, and now—for practically the first time in his forty years—he felt the true essence of home.

The log cabin fit the scenery, and aside from indoor plumbing—a luxury in these parts—it was rustic and simple, the way he liked it. One story, a single bedroom, wood-beam vaulted ceiling, a bathroom he'd splurged extra on, and a front room with a kitchen nook and an open fire.

He wanted to sit back and pop open a beer, but he had people to see off and a new employee to greet.

Most of the staff, Pat and Nina included, were going back to Nome for the next few months that they were closed. Too little daylight and bad weather kept guests away. Plenty of folks traveled up here to spend the holidays in a winter wonderland, though January through March were dead.

Over the years, it had become Declan's favorite time at the Retreat. Pat and Nina spent that time promoting the place from their office in Nome, some of the staff had other jobs, and a select few stayed behind. Declan didn't have to be polite to anyone, no one complained about his grouchy mood, and his sister-in-law wasn't around to give pitying looks and sympathetic smiles.

This year, the group that would be here consisted of an electrician and two handymen Declan had recently hired, Sarah, who cleaned but also tended to the thirteen dogs that lived on the grounds, and the latest addition who'd be here any minute.

Reaching over to the low coffee table, Declan picked up the folder he kept with the employee information for the four new guys. Kyle, the electrician, had been here a couple weeks already, and John and Alex, the handymen, had arrived three days ago. Then there was Quinn Ward.

The first name never failed to make Declan's gut clench, except the last name didn't match, which was a goddamn good thing. Had it been a Quinn Sawyer, Declan would've checked out more than just work references. This Quinn was older than the one Declan remembered, not to mention he was an actual construction worker. Declan had spoken to the twenty-nine-year-old, admittedly impressed with his resume.

Declan himself had worked in construction all his adult life, but he'd never seen a war zone, that was for sure.

"It's time, little brother!" Pat hollered from outside.

Declan rolled his eyes and stood up. He was still dressed from his walk over to see Lola—his favorite Husky that happened to be expecting pups—only his boots and beanie missing. As he got to the small entryway, he ripped the door open and stuck his feet into his boots.

"Two minutes," he told Pat for the millionth time since they were kids. "You're *two* minutes older."

"Two minutes, two decades...what's the difference?" Pat smirked.

The wind howled outside, so Declan grabbed his beanie, zipped up his parka properly, and closed the door to keep the heat from escaping.

"Between you and me?" He side-eyed Pat. "The difference couldn't be bigger."

NORTHBOUND

Being Navy brats, Pat had embraced their lifestyle of never settling down. He'd lived for the next trip, the next time he got to pack the boxes that were never really unpacked in the first place, and enjoyed making new friends. Then ten years ago, he met Nina during a ski trip in Whistler, and he was done for. In the meantime, Declan had only ever wanted a quiet place where he felt at home. He didn't like taking risks, he was somewhat withdrawn and detached due to his past, and he'd been the first one to bail Pat out of any trouble when they were young before retreating to the shadows.

Even now, Declan played it safe. Pat often asked when Declan was gonna put his name on the paper and co-own the Retreat, and the answer was never. He'd probably never leave this place either, but he was perfectly content being the employed "fixer."

"True. You do have more grays than I do." Pat lifted his hat to offer a flash of his dark hair. Combined with their pale complexion, their hair appeared more black than brown. "If it makes you feel any better, you *look* older. But we both know I'm the wise one."

Declan snorted and pulled out his gloves from his pockets. "You keep telling yourself that, you vain motherfucker." He looked over to the airstrip to see Mitch's plane had landed. "I suppose it's time to meet the new kid."

Pat stopped and looked in the opposite direction, toward the three bigger buildings that framed the courtyard where they had barbecues when the weather allowed it. "You know what?" He scratched his cheek. "You go. I'll tell the others to get a damn move on. Nina's probably still running back and forth on our floor."

Declan had seen that several times already. Whenever it was time for their winter break, Nina took forever to pack. "I'll see you over there soon." He nodded. "You guys better hurry, though. The weather's only getting worse." He took a step, only to pause when a thought struck. "Want me to get your plane out of the hangar?"

They were already taking two planes, and it might save time if Declan helped.

"Nah, there's still time for that." Pat tightened his scarf and bunched up his shoulders against the cold.

Declan walked the path along the edge of the forest and reached the airstrip in a minute or two. Out there, in the open, the wind was a whole lot worse than on the Retreat grounds. Trees protected them from the worst when blizzards hit, which was why Pat and Nina had picked this spot to build the Retreat.

Coastal Alaska was mostly shrubby and bare, but a wildlife association had built a two-acre large—or small?—forest to offer more seclusion, hibernation spots, and food for animals. Then they'd relocated farther inland, leaving the land for sale for Pat and Nina.

Parked near the hangar, old Mitch was unloading boxes of supplies when Declan joined him.

"Long time, no see." Declan clapped him on the back and grabbed a crate. No trip was wasted, and this was to stock up on the food that would keep them all fed while they were up here. "Mainly your boy doing the runs now, eh?"

Mitch grunted, setting a box down on the ground. "Yeah. He tells me I'm getting old. Can you believe that?"

"Never." Declan chuckled. "So where's my new handyman?"

The wry look Mitch gave him was enough for Declan to groan. If the kid had thrown up, gotten scared, or hell, even thought he was gonna die…it wasn't good news. 'Cause if he got freaked about a short plane ride, how was he gonna react when he woke up and there was a bear outside the window? Or if the power went out? Or if they were out working and a wolf paid a visit?

So close to Bering Land Bridge, it happened often enough. The national preserve was packed with wildlife, as were the Retreat grounds.

A door swung open, and Declan saw two large duffel bags being dropped on the ground. Then a guy climbed down the steps on unsteady legs. Declan caught a peek of shaggy, light brown hair before the kid shuddered and pulled up the hood of his jacket.

Behind them, Mitch started carrying crates in the direction of the Retreat.

"I actually made it," Declan heard the kid mumble shakily.

NORTHBOUND

Declan frowned and squinted. Snow whirled around them, and Quinn was bundled up so only his eyes and a little of his cheeks were visible. But those eyes…and that *fucking* name…were messing with Declan's head.

Not to mention both Quinns were from Florida. The Quinn Declan had once known lived in Sarasota, and Miami was hardly far away.

"Quinn Ward?" Declan asked.

"Um." The guy shuffled closer with his bags. "About that…"

When only a few feet separated them, the kid lifted his gaze again, and Declan saw those green eyes. The ones that had haunted him for years in his dreams. Along with shame and revulsion.

"*You*." Accusation and disbelief laced Declan's voice, but he couldn't fucking help it.

CHAPTER 2

Oh, boy.

Quinn licked his lips nervously and fidgeted with the strap of one of his bags. "I can explain?" He wasn't supposed to phrase it as a question, but his focus was too trained on the man in front of him.

Quinn had always had a crush on Declan, though he'd hid it well. It was almost like a rite of passage: crush on a straight man. And at first, before Quinn had gotten to know Declan, it had been easy to blame it on simple attraction. Quinn found Declan's gruff exterior, his dark blue eyes, and all his contrasts irresistible. There was just something about a man who looked every bit of the trade he worked in. Men's men whose bodies had that solid build from years of hard work as opposed to hours spent in a gym.

"You can start right fucking now." Declan folded his arms across his chest, the black fabric of his parka just barely hiding the strength underneath. "Give me one reason not to put you on the plane and send you back to Florida, Quinn."

Quinn bristled at that because he didn't deserve Declan's treatment.

Coming here under false pretenses notwithstanding.

"You've always been stubborn. So if I'd called you," Quinn

began impatiently, "or emailed you—or visited under normal circumstances—would you have even acknowledged me?"

Declan's hard stare and heavy silence were answer enough, which *still* fucking hurt Quinn. He was sick and tired of being the black sheep at home without any reason he was aware of. And Declan was the key to figuring out why Quinn didn't have much civil family left other than his parents.

"Listen. I'm sorry about lyin', okay?" Quinn did his best to push down his frustrations. "If you're worried about the job, don't be. I may not be as skilled as Logan, but I'm not fucking clueless. I won't be a liability." *Much.*

"Logan. Logan Ward." Declan pinched the bridge of his nose. "Your old neighbor. I should've known. God*dammit*, I should've known."

"Yeah? You know what I should know?" Quinn stalked forward and pushed down his scarf a bit, pissed now. "I should know what I've done to make my family hate my guts." He poked hard at Declan's chest. "I deserve to know why my cousins won't speak to me, why my aunt claims I destroyed her, and why all this changed when *you* left Sarasota."

Declan's eyes widened at that. "She…she claims *what*?"

Quinn figured it was a rhetorical question, so he didn't repeat himself. Instead, he hiked up his duffels on his shoulders, his features tight with determination.

"I'm not leavin' until I find out why." That said, he grabbed a crate and began walking the way the pilot had headed.

It was cold as hell, the snow was coming down hard, and the wind chilled Quinn to the bones. He didn't care. He was staying. He'd asked everyone in his family what exactly had happened, and no one ever gave him answers.

His parents didn't know; otherwise, they definitely would've told him. Quinn was lucky in that respect. His folks were supportive and always there for him, but with the size of their family, the good was easily drowned out and replaced with reasons to leave. Which Quinn had done. Shortly after Declan disappeared, Quinn had moved to Miami where Logan had taken him in.

Quinn passed a bunch of log cabins and figured those were

the ones they'd be fixing up. The exteriors were all done, and he knew the plumbing, outside wiring, and insulation had been finished before winter.

Logan had given him countless books and research materials to study up on, stating it wouldn't be enough, but at least Quinn would know the difference between a screwdriver and a hammer now. *Hardy-har-har.* In truth, Quinn had worked on a construction site. Once. For two weeks.

This was different, though. He wouldn't have to deal with heavy machinery, day laborers who didn't speak English, and working around the clock to meet crazy deadlines.

As Quinn got closer to three massive versions of the log cabins, he spotted a group of people coming out of the eastern building. According to the brochure, that was the three-story house the staff lived in. The middle building also had three stories, and the western—the one for backpackers—had two.

The pilot was on his way back to the airstrip, though he'd left the shoveled path and was now greeting a pack of dogs behind the hostel-like building. There was a large adjacent kennel where the dogs presumably lived and a fenced yard for them to run around in. The pilot petted them through the fence and gave them treats.

A woman appeared from behind the shed, outside the fence, and she was walking a bunch of other dogs. How many did they have here?

Quinn grunted at the heaviness of the crate and his luggage and continued forward. The group that had exited the staff house was getting closer, and soon, Quinn was face-to-face with a carbon copy of Declan.

Quinn had heard of Patrick of course, but he'd never met him.

"You must be the new kid my brother hired. Quinn, right?" Patrick stuck out a gloved hand and grinned. "I'm Patrick, and this is my wife, Nina. Welcome to the Retreat."

"Thanks. Nice to meet you." Quinn moved the crate to support it on his hip so he could shake Patrick's hand. "You too, Nina." He smiled politely and nodded at the short woman next to Patrick. "You don't happen to know where I'm supposed to be, do you?"

"Oh, yeah." Patrick gestured at the staff house. "Second floor, third room to the right. That's yours. Your housemates are on the same floor."

Nina and Patrick gave him a quick rundown of the facilities and assured him the other guys would show him around. Then they wished Quinn good luck before they and a few others continued on their way.

Quinn hummed to himself as he trudged through the snow in the courtyard. He'd heard something about part of the staff leaving for the off-season; Declan had told Logan that during the phone interview, and Logan had passed on the message. Quinn hadn't really thought about it, but now he was curious. How many were sticking around these next three months?

He got the answer when he'd entered the building and kicked off his boots. A tall guy with tattoos covering his forearms and neck introduced himself as Kyle and took the crate from him, leaving it in the kitchen. He was in his early thirties, Quinn guessed, and then learned Kyle was an electrician. Born and raised in Barrow, wherever that was. John and Alex were handymen, cousins, and lived in Anchorage where they had wives and kids.

Quinn was a bit overwhelmed at the enthusiastic introductions, but he could imagine how easily it got lonely up here. Maybe he'd be eager to interact with just about anybody after a month or two here, as well.

"Come on, I'll show you your room." Kyle offered a friendly smile and grabbed one of Quinn's duffels. "Hmm...who did I forget...?" He took the lead and headed up the stairs. "Declan, of course. I assume you've met him."

"You could say that," Quinn muttered.

Kyle snickered. "I'm sure he was his usual grumpy self. Don't take it personal." Third room to the right. Kyle opened the door to Quinn's home for the next three months. "Then there's Sarah. She cleans here full time, but her passion is taking care of the dogs. Don't treat her like a maid, though. I got an earful when I forgot to clean up my breakfast one morning." He smirked and stepped aside so Quinn could pass. "Full of fire, that one."

The room was small but would fit just fine. Quinn dropped his bags on the queen-sized bed and sat down, taking off his jacket and pushing down his snow pants, leaving him in his thermal wear and hoodie. There was a closet and a dresser for his clothes, a nightstand for his personal belongings, and a desk where he could set up his laptop.

"I plan on asking her out," Kyle said and rubbed the back of his neck.

"Message received." Quinn's mouth tugged up, and he lifted a brow. "She's not my type, anyway. I'm gay."

Kyle hadn't seen that coming, Quinn could tell. The tatted electrician appeared stunned for a moment, and then he straightened. "*Really?*"

Quinn almost laughed at Kyle's comical expression. It was better than hatred, no doubt, though now he kind of hoped this Sarah girl found a better dude. Because Kyle looked *interested*.

Bisexual horndog…or an Alaskan in the closet?

Kyle was an attractive bad boy-looking guy, except Quinn wasn't here to hook up. He didn't get laid much at home either, and anyone who'd been in Miami knew there were plenty of fish in the gayest sea of them all.

Quinn preferred relationships over one-nighters, his online interactions over socializing in real life, nature over nightclubs, and running along the beach over cruising for tail.

"Not gonna happen, my man," he told Kyle with an easy smile. "I'm flattered, but I'm not interested."

Unfortunately, Kyle seemed to like a challenge.

*

After saying all his goodbyes and finding storage for their food, Declan disappeared into his cabin. He wanted to clear his goddamn head; unfortunately, it was noon, which meant the sun had risen and they had daylight for the next four or so hours. While there'd be no work done today, he should at least round up the guys and give them the schedule for the week.

Too bad he felt like shit.

Guilt weighed on his shoulders, heavier than ever. He didn't know how to even begin to process Quinn's being here, much less what the kid had told him. One thing was clear, though. Declan had to push his own issues aside and be there for Quinn. If the Sawyers, mainly Quinn's aunt Lynn, had found a scapegoat in Quinn, it was Declan's fault.

Well, actually, Lynn was being an unreasonable cunt, but that was nothing new.

Figuring he might as well get this over with, Declan grabbed his planner, the blueprints for Kyle, and his radio. Then he trekked up toward the staff house, passing Sarah on the way. She followed her own schedule, so she didn't have to suffer through this meeting.

"Everything good?" he asked, slowing down a little.

"Yeah, boss." She grinned at him and didn't stop shoveling snow inside the fence. Seven or eight Huskies saw the shoveling more as a game, so they chased her around and tried to wrestle with the shovel. "I saw the new guy. He's cute."

He's also gay.

A blessing and a curse all at once.

Quinn being gay made it all the more difficult to let go of certain fixations, although Declan had sure as hell done a decent job—most of the time—since he'd left Florida. Even after six years, he was still disgusted with himself for what he'd done.

CHAPTER 3

Quinn found an unlikely friend in Alex, the Hulk-sized handyman who'd spent the first twenty minutes of their initial meeting talking about sports and brewing his own beer. Then when Quinn had mentioned none of that was really for him and that he preferred gaming, Alex had lit up like a Christmas tree. Apparently, gaming was even better than hockey.

Alex was on kitchen duty for the day, so Quinn helped out while they discussed the pros and cons of DayZ, an online zombie game.

Everyone was dressed in thermal wear indoors, so Quinn hadn't bothered to change out of his. It was probably a good thing he didn't find any of the men hot enough to elicit a reaction his body-hugging thermals would never be able to hide.

When John joined them, they switched to a more neutral topic: the weather.

Quinn would find it mind-numbingly boring if it weren't for all the questions he had. "So this whole midnight sun thing's just a myth?" 'Cause the two days he'd spent in Nome before flying up here had given him a total of eight hours of daylight.

A bit different from sunny Florida.

"'Course not." Alex chuckled as he mashed potatoes with

butter by the stove. "But it's in the summer. The winter's all about darkness."

Oh. Quinn felt stupid.

Still, this was a whole new world from what he was used to. In the past two days, he'd found out that Alaska was colder than anything he could've imagined, groceries were expensive, Eskimos were real, many towns in the state weren't even connected by roads, and did he mention the cold?

As the front door opened down in the hallway, Quinn turned to John, who'd said he enjoyed hunting, and asked, "Have you ever seen polar bears?"

John lifted his gaze from the fishing magazine he was reading and smiled. "Sure. They're not that common in this area, though."

"Good." Quinn didn't wanna worry about those.

"The biggest bears aren't always the worst."

Quinn's head whipped around, and he saw Declan standing in the doorway, removing his parka.

John agreed. "Watch out for the black bears instead. Irritable as fuck. Especially if they don't hibernate."

Quinn was having a difficult time focusing. John, Kyle, and Alex in thermals was one thing. He hadn't fucking considered Declan.

He should've. He really should've.

Declan used to keep his dark hair buzzed short. It was a couple inches longer now. Messy, hot. His muscles seemed more defined now, too. His reddish tourist tan was long gone, bringing back the contrasts Quinn remembered from when Declan had just moved to Sarasota from Chicago. Icy and clear, dark blue eyes. *Shit.* His dark green thermals hugged his muscular thighs. They were pretty much the same height, though Declan was certainly larger.

Declan was also oblivious to Quinn's staring—thank fuck. Catching himself, Quinn spun around to slice some more carrots. In the meantime, Declan sat at the table with John and discussed something about the cabin bathrooms.

"Smells good in here." Kyle entered the kitchen and sat down too, but not before giving Quinn a sly wink.

Quinn rolled his eyes and withheld a smirk.

"Aaand there we go. I get it now." Alex grinned at the fish he was now putting in a pan. It sizzled and popped in the oil. "I'll take the carrots when you're ready."

Quinn frowned and handed the cutting board with the sliced carrots to Alex. "Get what?"

"Your deal." Alex kept his voice low. "The way you eyed the boss made me curious." *Dammit.* "But if Kyle's sniffed you out already, it can only mean you bat for the other team."

"Ah." Quinn didn't quite know what to say. "Yeah. Born and raised with the gay *deal*." He was curious about Kyle, though. "So, I'm guessin' no closet for him, huh?"

Alex snorted. "He'll take it all—with anyone. Beds, kitchen tables, sheds…closets too, I suppose."

Unable to help himself, Quinn cracked up a bit. And his question about Kyle had been answered. Bisexual horndog it was.

*

As soon as lunch was served, Declan occupied his mind with work. Instead of thinking about Quinn's tight ass and swimmer's body, he spoke to John about the bathrooms they'd focus on the first month. Instead of fantasizing about fisting Quinn's sun-streaked hair while they fucked, he handed out a list of supplies and tools they'd find in the workshop behind the main house. Instead of letting an irrational surge of jealousy control him after witnessing Kyle flirt with Quinn, Declan discussed indoor heating with Alex.

Quinn had changed drastically since he was nineteen, and it was taking all of Declan's willpower not to let his mind wander.

The kid grew up.

"Why aren't you going with underfloor heating? I know it's not optimal for wood flooring, but it'll look better." Alex pointed at the blueprints on the table. "Or is the gap between the foundation and the beams too big?"

That was partly the reason. Without the concrete right there to provide a better heat transfer, it would take too long to heat up the cabin. It was also money. "Too expensive, and we don't have time for the extra pipework. Plus, the wiring for radiators has already been drawn. We just gotta install them." Declan shoveled some fried fish and gravy into his mouth. "The bathrooms have heated floors, though."

"Water-based or electric mats?" Kyle asked.

"Water-based," Declan replied. "It was the best option without elevating the floor too much." He flicked a glance at Quinn and didn't know whether to laugh or curse. Quinn was undoubtedly overwhelmed and confused by the talk, which Declan had known was gonna happen. He cleared his throat and cut into another piece of fish. "Quinn, you'll be working with me." He honestly didn't trust anybody else with the guy, especially not if the others believed Quinn was actually experienced with this.

Quinn's head snapped up. "Oh? Um, all right."

Declan moved on, not wanting to make a big deal out of it. "Kyle, tomorrow I need you to check the insulation before we install the radiators. Make sure it's tight."

"Got it." Kyle nodded firmly. "You don't think the construction crew did a good job?"

"More like they may not have been used to working in this climate," Declan answered. "Pat hired cheap labor from the Lower 48 before I could interfere, and I couldn't get us out of the contract." He chugged down some milk. "I stopped watching them like a hawk when they doubled up on the insulation under the floor, though. I think it's fine—just wanna be sure."

Kyle nodded again, and then John inquired about the fireplaces that would, despite the plans for radiators, provide most heat.

*

Quinn was screwed.

After lunch, he ran up to his room and brought out all the books Logan had given him. The crash course hadn't been enough, so now he was gonna try to drill the instructions into his fucking skull.

With a marker dangling between his lips, he paced the floor

and flipped through the pages of a book of terminology. Later when he received his belt, new boots, and utility pants, he wanted to know everything about them. Well, not the clothes. The tools, on the other hand...

He recognized most of it; then when it came to picking the right tool for a certain task, he wanted to punch himself in the throat.

He was looking up insulation and air infiltration barriers when there was a knock on the door.

"Come in," Quinn muttered, not looking up from the text he was reading.

There was a chuckle from the doorway. "Why am I not surprised to find you studying?"

Quinn stiffened and struggled to hide his embarrassment. Dragging his gaze away from the book, he took the marker out of his mouth and looked up at Declan leaning casually against the doorframe.

"I don't wanna fuck up," Quinn admitted with a frown. "I *won't.*"

"Takes a stubborn man to know one." Declan smiled as if he were remembering something from Florida. Maybe he was. "Good trait to have up here, I suppose." His smile morphed into a grin, and he scratched his nose. "How're you finding Alaska so far?"

Quinn huffed. "Frigid."

"Eh. Probably colder in Minnesota right now." Declan walked farther into the room and dropped a plastic bag on the bed. "There's everything you'll need for tomorrow. I'll get you the keys to a sled, too."

What in the ever-loving fuck. "A sled?" Quinn had a vision of dogs taking him places.

"A snowmachine," Declan clarified.

"Like a snowmobile?"

Declan smiled wryly. "Sure. Lower-48'ers call 'em that."

About that. Quinn had heard that term before, most recently over lunch. He'd heard it a couple times in Nome, too. "What exactly is the Lower 48?"

"Shouldn't take long for you to figure that out," Declan

responded, amused. It made the corners of his eyes crinkle, and why the hell did Quinn find that sexy? "It's a place in the world where everyone thinks Texas is big. It's cute, really."

It dawned on Quinn, and he couldn't help but laugh. That was clever. And a bit snarky. Okay, so the continental US states were called the Lower 48. He wondered idly what other local terms he'd pick up here, but then something hit him.

He narrowed his eyes at Declan. "You can't have lived here more than six years. Since when does that give you the right to knock the rest of us, huh?"

"I was *born* here." Declan gave him a strange look. "You didn't know that?"

No, Quinn hadn't known. "I thought you were a Navy brat."

"I am. Even those are born somewhere," Declan pointed out. "We moved away early—when I was nine or ten—and I didn't come back until six years ago, but I was born in Kodiak."

"Huh." Quinn didn't know what else to say. Although…getting them on to the right track held appeal. "You know, maybe if you'd stuck around, I would've learned that about you."

It stung that Declan had left without a single word.

"Subtle." Declan raised a brow before he sighed and looked down, frowning. "What you said before—you're right. You deserve to know." He didn't look comfortable with the notion, though. "Mind giving me some time to work up to it? It's not a story I'm proud of."

Quinn nodded hesitantly. "Of course." He just couldn't understand what could've happened back then to cause such a clusterfuck. Or how it involved Quinn. "I have three months." He smiled a little to ease the tension.

Declan appeared grateful. "It's really good to see you again, kid."

That caused a sliver of warmth to creep up Quinn's spine. Despite the "kid" nonsense. "I'm not a kid anymore, you know."

Both of Declan's brows rose, and he chuckled before he turned to leave. "Don't I know it." He paused in the doorway and tapped the frame, giving Quinn one more glance. "I'll ease you into things when we get to work, but for now, don't walk outside alone without protection. We do have a lot of wildlife around here."

Terrific. Quinn swallowed, suddenly nervous.

CHAPTER 4

Two weeks later, Quinn hurt. *Everywhere.*

Sarah was fixing dinner, so Quinn—with his proverbial tail between his legs—retreated to his room on the second floor to moan in misery.

The soreness, the constant ache... Christ, there were muscles he didn't even know he had that throbbed with pain.

His ego was wounded, too. The other men were able to do a whole lot more, yet they didn't look like they were ready to keel over. Today, Quinn had carried brand-new toilets from the main house to each cabin, which had been followed by ten mirrors and ten sinks. And no matter how padded the knees of his pants were, the previous day when they'd worked on tiling where the bathtubs would go, his kneecaps hurt to the point where he kind of wanted to call Mom to come get him.

He wanted to call Logan too, and since he was stuck in Iraq, Quinn had to wait until Logan contacted him.

Cons: He was so tired by the end of each day that he had barely opened his laptop since he got here. Kyle's flirting was getting tedious. They ate too much Spam in Alaska. The lack of daylight hours was slightly depressing. Fresh produce was hard to come by, and whatever couldn't be frozen was going bad at this point.

Pros: Alaska was fucking beautiful. Declan was funny and easy to talk to, and working together with him made it worth all the pain.

They were basically picking up where they'd left off six years ago in Florida. They'd started as acquaintances who merely greeted each other whenever Aunt Lynn brought her new boyfriend around, and then they'd been on and off for some time. Declan had even left once for a job in Fort Lauderdale and hadn't returned for two years.

When Quinn turned eighteen, he and Declan got to talking at one family dinner. Quinn couldn't remember the topic, only that it grew from there. They sought each other out at each gathering, then exchanged emails and became friends on social media and then met up for coffee here and there.

Because of the friendship, Quinn hadn't found it too difficult to hide his attraction for Declan—or the feelings that were developing. It wasn't often Quinn connected with people, so he wanted to cherish their friendship.

Then one day, Declan was just gone and Aunt Lynn came over to curse Quinn to the fiery pits of hell.

Content to know he'd find out the truth soon enough, Quinn slumped down on his bed and grinned to himself. *Declan's back in my life*, he thought.

Their age gap made itself known often, though it was never a bad thing. They just gave each other new perspectives and more to talk about. Also, was it okay to find the fifteen years separating them hot?

"Dinner's ready, boys!" Sarah shouted from downstairs.

Quinn wanted to cry. Could his legs even carry him downstairs?

*

Declan closed the door to his bedroom to give Lola privacy. The Husky showed signs of labor, so when Sarah radioed him to say dinner was ready, he told her he'd skip it. What with it being

Lola's second litter, he wasn't worried, but he wanted to stay close just in case.

Sarah replied that she'd be there later and that she'd bring food.

And when "later" came around, so did Quinn.

Fuck my life.

"I've never seen a dog give birth," Quinn said, taking off his gloves. His cheeks were flushed from the cold, and happiness brightened his green eyes. "I've heard puppies are blind when they're born. Is that true?"

Declan let Sarah answer while he got another fill of Quinn's youthful excitement and beauty.

On the one hand, it was incredible to have Quinn here. On the other…Declan's feelings were returning with a vengeance, and that could never be a good thing because his downright nasty fantasies reappeared as well.

The sweeter Quinn was, the dirtier Declan's thoughts became.

Accepting his plate with a thank you, Declan took off the plastic on his way to his kitchenette and placed the food in the microwave for a bit.

Sarah tiptoed to the door leading to his bedroom and pressed her ear to the wood. She smiled widely and nodded at Declan, which he assumed meant Lola was in labor.

Behind them, Quinn sat down on the couch with a soft groan, and when Declan turned, the kid was rubbing his heel.

Declan stifled a smirk. He knew Quinn was in pain but was mostly too proud to show it.

He'd done a good job so far, Declan had to admit. As long as Quinn stayed away from the more complicated tasks, there was no reason to think they wouldn't be ready in time.

Declan threw some wood on the fire in the corner before he grabbed his plate and sat down next to Quinn on the couch. He was starving, and Sarah was without a doubt the best cook at the Retreat right now.

"So, it's Friday," Quinn mentioned casually. "We worked last weekend. Some time off wouldn't hurt, you know. Just a suggestion."

Declan thought about fucking with him, then opted against it in the end. "We have to finish the bathroom we started today, but that'll only take a couple hours. After that, you bet, kid." He chewed and swallowed the heavenly perfection that was Sarah's beer-battered halibut and looked back to see Quinn's tired smile and closed eyes. "I even have a surprise for you guys."

It had been Nina's idea to give the men something extra at the end of each week, except they'd been busy last weekend. However, tomorrow Declan would open up the pool area in the main house. They'd eat in the dining room, too, and finish with some poker where coveted candy bars worked as currency.

"I'm too exhausted to ask," Quinn chuckled drowsily. "Wake me up when the puppies are here."

Stop being so goddamn boyish and sweet.

Not a single smile was forced when it came to Quinn. The guy made Declan feel alive again, but that wasn't the issue. It was the gutter his mind fell into whenever he was alone that was the problem.

For instance, Declan had learned that Quinn liked watching cartoons on Saturday mornings. And Declan's thought had been, *"Seems like something you could do while nursing from my cock."*

Yeah. One pervert coming right up.

God knew there were plenty of freaks out there, and Declan's fantasies paled in comparison to many. But the reactions he'd received from partners in the past hadn't been positive unless kinky sex was all they wanted from him.

Between that and the last time Declan had lost control of his imagination, he'd become resigned to a life alone.

*

Quinn was having the hottest dream when he was woken up by a hand on his shoulder. He blinked slowly, remembering where he was, and saw Declan squatting down in front of him.

"You wanted to see the pups?" he asked quietly.

Quinn yawned and nodded at the same time. Yeah, he wanted to see the little things. "Lead the way, boss." *Ugh.* His legs ached as he hauled his ass off the couch. He stretched, cringing at the sound of his bones cracking and popping. "Where's Sarah?" He yawned again.

"She just left." Declan led the way to the bedroom. "She stuck around to weigh the pups and make sure they were equally strong."

Quinn made a face. At dinner, Sarah had told them what sometimes happened if a puppy was too weak to nurse from its mother.

"Lola only lets me and Sarah touch her right now, so keep your distance a little," Declan murmured, opening the door to the bedroom. It was warm in here. "She wouldn't bite, but she gets restless and worried."

Quinn averted his eyes from the large bed in the middle of the room and saw a Husky lying in a makeshift dog bed behind the door with a bunch of towels. Then, as he leaned closer, he saw five tiny puppies sleeping by her belly.

Quinn was sold. The puppies weren't all that cute if he was being honest, but still. The whole experience was pretty fucking cool.

"What're you gonna name them?" he whispered.

Declan smiled. "I don't know yet. You wanna name one?"

Quinn peered over at Declan with wide eyes. "I can do that?"

"Of course." Declan chuckled softly. "I actually think Sarah's running out of names. With these new ones, we have eighteen of them."

Quinn grinned and looked at the sleeping puppies again. He'd have to come up with a kick-ass name as soon as he'd decided which puppy was his favorite.

"When do they start runnin' around?" he asked.

Declan hummed. "It'll be a while—couple weeks at least. I don't know how city folk do it. Out here, we leave a lot to the mother in the beginning."

Quinn was glad he still had a lot of time left in Alaska.

A while later, they left the bedroom again, and Declan dropped his duvet and pillows on the couch.

"You're sleeping out here?" Quinn wondered. "That can't be comfortable."

"It's a pullout. And it's just the first couple nights so Lola can have some privacy. But not yet. I think the lights are out."

Quinn frowned as Declan walked over to a window and peered out. There were two lamps working just fine in the front room, so he had no idea what Declan was talking about.

"Yep." Declan headed to the entryway and started putting on his snow pants and parka. "This is probably new for you, so come on."

Quinn glanced out the window on his way to get dressed, only to freeze and do a double take. Holy shit. *Lights!* The Northern Lights. *The lights are out.* Excitement buzzed in Quinn's veins, and he was in a hurry all of a sudden.

It was so cold outside that the tiny hairs in his goddamn nostrils froze, but Quinn couldn't have cared less. Once the beanie and gloves were on, he stood on the small porch and looked up at the sky.

Neon green splashed across the clear sky in an electric spectacle, some wavy streaks bluish and some yellowish.

"Oh my God. This is…" Quinn was speechless. *Breathtaking. Amazing. Beyond beautiful.*

*

Declan side-eyed Quinn while the colors danced across the night sky.

Whatever word Quinn wanted to use for the lights, Declan wanted to use for Quinn.

Goddamn, Declan really missed companionship.

At one point, he had stayed in a relationship with a woman he didn't care for solely to remain close to this then nineteen-year-old guy. Yet even back then, Quinn had been incredibly smart and mature. When he found an interest, he latched on to it and refused to let go until he knew everything there was to know. And it seemed every time Declan saw him back then, there was a new interest Quinn was eager to discuss.

Aside from his profession, Declan was more the type who knew a little about a lot, whereas Quinn did the opposite. He was intense.

"How did you get here tonight?" Declan was prepared to walk Quinn back to the house, though he was almost sure he'd taken the sled. Despite the short walk, snow and wildlife made the sled an easy choice.

"Sled." Quinn never looked away from the sky. "Parked behind your cabin."

Declan followed his gaze and let out a sigh of contentment. Didn't matter how long someone had lived in Alaska. The lights never got old.

The silence was comfortable. Everything was still and peaceful. The moment was perfect, especially with Declan's mind being quiet.

John was probably asleep, otherwise they'd hear him whistling to himself across the courtyard by now.

*

The morning after, Quinn worked like the Energizer Bunny so he could have the weekend off later. Standing in the front room of one of the cabins, he prepared the last batch of ceramic mixing adhesive for the tiles while Declan took measurements for the accent tiles that would go above the bathtub.

Quinn would rather be in the bathroom, because this wasn't their first cabin. He knew exactly what he'd see in there right this second. Declan wearing his work pants with all those utility pockets and his tool belt, a snug T-shirt hugging his torso, dust and stains here and there… Muscles flexing. Perspiration glistening. Concentration furrowing his brow. A couple days worth of scruff. And he'd be on his knees where the bathtub would go.

Last night after watching the Northern Lights together, Quinn had been unable to sleep before getting off in the shower, and if Declan kept this up, Quinn could see that becoming a daily task.

"You almost ready, Quinn?" Declan called.

Oh, right. Quinn finished the mixing and brought it to the bathroom, and there he was. Declan on his knees.

"Here." Quinn cleared his throat and looked away.

"Thanks, kid." Declan accepted the batch. "You can throw this away." Quinn flicked his eyes at the silicone tube Declan extended and grabbed it. "While I wrap this up, you can do an inventory of the bathroom supplies."

Quinn nodded in understanding and then exited the cabin, putting on his parka on the way to his snowmachine. He was fairly certain he'd seen a wolverine lurking in the forest behind the main house, so Quinn rarely ventured outside without the vehicle. Plus, it was convenient for paths where they hadn't shoveled in a while.

He had to admit being up here in Alaska was…fun. The endless layers of clothing were a drag, but he was getting used to it. When he thought about it, he also had to admit he enjoyed his job. He definitely hadn't seen *that* coming.

CHAPTER 5

But time off beat everything else, Quinn decided early that afternoon. Because when Declan opened the massive basement in the main house, Quinn could see himself never leaving. *Holy fuck*. It was gorgeous. Dimly lit and with the same rustic feel as the rest of the place, the pool area was about to become one of the favorites.

"This is what I'm talking about," Alex said with a wide smile.

"Fancy." Kyle's brows lifted. "Here I was, thinking it couldn't get better than indoor plumbing."

The pool wasn't huge, but it was big enough to do laps, had three lanes, and one shallow end and one deep.

While Kyle and Alex stripped down to boxers and dove in, John—being closer to Declan's age—went to change in to trunks.

Quinn smiled back at Declan. "So this is the spa, huh?"

"Not all of it," Declan replied. "We redid the attic and installed a skylight a few years back for the masseuse and wellness therapist, or whatever Nina calls it. They also do that weird thing where they put rocks on your back. Apparently mud on your face and salt scrubs are good for ya."

Quinn laughed and pulled off his scarf and gloves. The humidity made it feel like home, and he really wanted to jump in. "You not goin' in the water?"

"Later." Declan smiled and jerked a thumb over his shoulder. "Sarah and I are making fish tacos for dinner in the restaurant, so I'll save the swimming 'til after."

At least Quinn would get to see Declan soaking wet and almost naked at some point. Good enough. "Want any help?" *Please say no.*

Declan snorted a chuckle. "Thanks for the offer, kid. But I can see you're itching to go in."

He was. He really, really was.

*

"Last one." Sarah smiled ruefully and handed Declan the last cucumber they'd eat for a while. "I feel like I should say something."

Declan shook his head, amused, and started dicing the cucumber. With their last meal containing fresh—somewhat fresh, anyway—vegetables, it was gonna be a feast.

The small, state-of-the-art chef's kitchen behind the dining room had its storage rooms and freezers packed with canned goods, preserves, baking supplies, meat, powdered dairy products, and countless other items, but it sort of paled at the sight of the counter between Declan and Sarah. The workstation was filled with bowls of chopped, diced, and sliced vegetables.

"I've noticed something these past couple of weeks," Sarah mentioned as she shredded a block of cheddar. "You're not as antisocial and grumpy anymore. You seem…happier."

"Oh?" Declan grinned and found a bowl for the cucumber bits. "Maybe because I am."

"I *knew* it." Sarah wagged the block of cheese at him. "So, who is it? I doubt it's Kyle, although that would make things easier for me. Thinks with his dick, that one…" She tapped her chin. "My bet is on Quinn."

Declan neither confirmed nor denied. It *was* Quinn, though nothing would happen in the way Sarah implied.

"Does he know you're interested?" Sarah went on.

No.

Quinn didn't even know Declan liked men, much less preferred them.

Declan had messed around with both genders in his late teens and twenties before he'd met a woman he spent the next four years with. They'd lived together in Chicago then eventually drifted apart, and Declan headed south, having never felt at home in Illinois. He still found men a lot more appealing; however, he'd never been able to go on attraction alone. There had to be more than that, and it was easier to connect with women. Until Quinn.

When they first met, Quinn was an awkward, lanky kid. He definitely didn't stick out in the crowd of Sawyers. That would've been fucked up, seeing as Quinn was only sixteen or something at the time. Not that it mattered. Declan and Lynn broke up because he'd been offered a job in Fort Lauderdale. Besides, she'd gotten frustrating. Everything was about her. A more egocentric woman was hard to come by.

Eventually though, Declan found himself back in Sarasota, and a night of drinking and loneliness led to them starting over. They dated casually on and off, although Lynn certainly pressured for more. Declan agreed to go to a family dinner with her, and the plan had been to break things off completely afterward. If only he hadn't run into Quinn, who had not only matured in the intervening two years, but they'd shared a common interest in Stephen King novels.

Declan shook his head to himself and began preparing the fish.

One thing had led to another. They slowly built a friendship that made Declan come back for more, and as time went on, attraction got in the way. By that point, several in Lynn's family considered him an honorary Sawyer. He couldn't imagine the tension if he ended it with her but stayed for Quinn. As friends— possibly. Though, how long could that last? Declan would only want more, and eventually Quinn would find someone.

Declan had resigned himself to leave, yet he kept stalling.

Then the decision was made for him when Lynn got slapped in the face by the truth one night.

He left and cut all ties with Quinn. No more online chats, new email address and phone number, no word of where he'd gone.

Declan wondered how Quinn had tracked him down, but Declan couldn't ask until he was ready to give something back, and *that* was a day he dreaded.

*

While Sarah set one of the tables in the dining room, Declan headed down to the basement and told the guys in the pool dinner was ready. Then he walked up the stairs again before he could see Quinn getting out of the water.

Declan didn't need the image.

It turned out to be futile, though. When the men joined Declan and Sarah, they'd barely dressed. Kyle was the worst, only wearing a towel around his narrow hips, showing off a tattooed torso and defined muscles. Quinn and John weren't much better, the only addition to the towels being T-shirts.

"The Sunshine State kid here knows how to swim." John clapped Quinn on the back and sat down at the round table. "This looks great."

"I almost beat you that last round," Kyle told Quinn.

"Only in your dreams, Kyle." Quinn smiled at Declan and sat down next to him. "You wanna have a go after dinner?" Water dripped from his hair, dampening the collar of his white T-shirt. "We could make it interestin'."

Declan forced himself to pretend to be casual and at ease.

"Hey, now." Kyle pointed a fork at Quinn. "I'd swim faster if the stakes were higher."

"I'm sure you would." Quinn focused on his food instead.

If Declan didn't know any better, he'd say Quinn was irritated with Kyle, which made Declan wonder if Kyle's flirting had advanced. If it had, he'd make sure to have a talk with Kyle later.

"This really does look amazing." Quinn nudged his elbow to Declan's. "I thought we ran out of fresh vegetables."

"We saved some for tonight," Sarah said with a wink.

Declan nodded and opened his beer. "So dig in, boys. Next piece of lettuce you'll see is when Pat and Nina return."

NORTHBOUND

*

Quinn had always been a lightweight when it came to anything alcoholic, so after three beers, he had a nice buzz going on. Nothing that affected his ability to beat everyone in swimming—just enough to make him feel a little bolder.

He whooped when he resurfaced, having beaten Kyle for the second time.

He was now two Milky Ways richer.

"Show me the chocolate, little cousin!" John hollered and made a gimme motion at Alex. They must've made a bet on the side.

Declan's plan had been poker, but when he revealed two boxes of chocolate bars, the game had changed. No one complained, and next up was Declan himself.

The man dove into the water, looking like sin in trunks, and Quinn left a grumpy Kyle behind.

"Make sure you rest, kid." Declan smirked. "I don't want any lame excuses when I win."

In response, Quinn flipped him the bird. "Bring it, *old man*."

Sarah giggled, sitting on the edge with her feet in the water. "Are we good on trash talk?"

I guess. Quinn swam under the line that divided their two lanes and got ready. He took a few deep breaths and rolled his shoulders. In the meantime, Declan just waited.

"Stakes?" Sarah asked.

Quinn had some Snickers he could get rid of, so he suggested, "Three Snickers bars for three of your Twix?"

Declan was undeterred. "Sure." He shrugged. "Or, you know, we could up the ante a bit."

Quinn laughed on the inside. He had this. Born and raised in Florida—come on. He practically lived in the water.

"Oooh." Alex rubbed his hands together from the side of the pool. "My money's on Quinn this time."

"That's fine with me." John, the traitor, was apparently betting on Declan. "You want in on this, Kyle?"

While Kyle said yes, Quinn tilted his head at Declan. "What

do you suggest?"

Declan's mouth tugged up. "You win, you can take all the candy bars you want. I win...? You take over kitchen duty for me three times and clean my bedroom. The pups aren't exactly housebroken."

Damn. That was some bet. Quinn bit his lip, deliberating. He wondered what made Declan so cocky. The man *knew* Quinn was a great swimmer, for Christ's sake.

"Deal," he said in the end. They shook on it.

"Okay, guys. On your mark," Sarah announced. Quinn gripped the edge and faced forward, his feet ghosting along the wall. "Ready...set...go!"

Quinn dipped underwater and pushed himself off the wall with force, slicing through the water with perfect ease.

*

Declan knew very well he couldn't beat Quinn.

Unless he was willing to play dirty, and Declan certainly was. There was even a memory from Florida that fueled him, and it was time for payback. So half a second after Quinn was off, Declan pushed away from the wall too, but he didn't stay in his own lane. Instead, he resurfaced right behind Quinn, and he heard the others laughing.

Any second now, Declan's strength would lose against Quinn's skill and stamina, so Declan sucked in a quick breath on the next freestyle stroke. Then he sped up and managed to grab on to Quinn's foot. With all his strength, he pulled Quinn back as much as he could, and then he passed the coughing and spluttering sunshine kid.

Declan could barely stop himself from laughing in the water.

Having no leverage but the bottom of the pool, Quinn was never able to catch up, and Declan was declared the winner by a guffawing Sarah across the pool.

"What the fuck!" Quinn slapped his hands against the surface when he finally reached the edge. He wiped water from his face and glared at Declan. "You should be disqualified for that shit!"

Declan laughed *hard*, feeling younger and more carefree than he had in ages.

"I'm serious!" Quinn's ego must've taken a big hit.

Down to chuckles, Declan closed the distance between them. "Not so fast, Quinn. Remember what you told me when you cheated and beat me in that video game in Sarasota?"

Welcome to Florida, bitch.

Judging by the wide-eyed expression Quinn suddenly had, he remembered.

"There you go." Declan leaned close, his hands brushing along Quinn's hips, and whispered in his ear. "Welcome to Alaska, bitch."

Quinn shuddered violently and backed away, quickly plastering a scowl on his handsome face. "You suck." Then he swam away.

Declan grinned, damn pleased with himself.

*

By the time Quinn had simmered down and left the pool, Sarah called it a night and reminded the guys to make sure they were completely dry before venturing outside. She also told Declan she'd take out Lola for him.

John wanted to call his wife, so he followed soon after.

Alex hauled himself out of the water and grabbed a towel. "I don't have a hot Skype date with my wifey until tomorrow, so how about some poker now?"

"Count me in," Kyle said.

Quinn looked over at Declan, who was already watching him. It appeared Declan was leaving it to Quinn to answer.

"I'm in." Quinn slid his gaze away from Declan, not ready for the night to be over. "I wouldn't mind getting back at the boss."

Declan was the last to leave the pool, and he merely smirked at Quinn.

Fifteen minutes later, they'd gathered in the bar upstairs and found a deck of cards and plenty of drinks.

Everyone presented their share of candy bars, and they had

even more to play with when Declan handed out little bags of peanuts and pillow chocolates. Once they'd decided what each item was worth, the four players put their game faces on.

"Would've been more interesting if we played for favors." Kyle winked at Quinn, who rolled his eyes.

Declan gritted his teeth.

Quinn gulped down some of his whiskey. "Like I've told you a dozen times, you're not my type." He grimaced and rubbed his chest. "Damn, that shit's strong."

Kyle leaned forward and popped open a soda for himself. "Who *is* your type?"

Declan dealt the cards for the first round, and he would've ordered Kyle to shut the fuck up if it weren't for the fact that he wanted to hear Quinn's answer.

"Not you," Quinn said, emphasizing both words.

Alex snickered and thumped Kyle on the back. "Looks like you're two for two, buddy. First Sarah shot you down, now Quinn. How will you live?"

"I don't get it." Kyle seemed honestly shocked. "I usually get what I want."

"Not this time." Declan's voice held enough warning for Kyle to get it. And if it didn't, the look in Declan's eyes did. "I'll only tell you once, we clear?"

"Got it, boss." Kyle folded. In more than one way. His cards hit the table, and he took a swig from his soda.

Under the table, a foot linked with Declan's, and he looked to his left in surprise to see Quinn giving him a small smile of thanks.

Satisfaction and yearning coursed through Declan.

Even more so when Quinn didn't withdraw his foot. It stayed there, wedged between Declan's while they played.

*

It was almost two in the morning when Quinn decided he'd had enough to drink. Alex had turned out to be a hilarious drunk, and Quinn laughed at Alex's dirty jokes until he had to wheeze for air.

Declan chuckled and patted Quinn on the back playfully. "You okay there? You need air, you know." The patting turned into stroking as Quinn tried to calm down. "Perhaps that's enough jokes from you, Alex." He smirked, and his hand went away, only to land on Quinn's leg under the table. "The sunshine kid can't handle it." *Squeeze.*

"I can handle it j-just fine." Quinn noticed a slight slur to his voice, which only made him laugh more. "If you're tired, go to bed, *old frontier.*" He found Declan's hand on his thigh and squeezed back. "Don't make it about me and what I can and can't handle."

Alex chuckled, almost as drunk as Quinn. "Old frontier… That's clever. 'Cause Alaska's known as the last—"

Kyle's and Quinn's groans cut him off.

"It stops being funny when you explain it, man!" Quinn complained.

Declan grinned and shook his head. "Maybe that's enough for one night."

"I knew it!" Quinn didn't remove his hand completely, though he slid it away so they just brushed together. "The boss needs his beauty sleep."

"Fuck it, so do I." Alex threw back a final shot before standing up. "If I know my kids, they'll call and wake me up at seven."

"I should go, too," Kyle said. "I'm heading out for a hunt tomorrow morning."

Seemed everyone was tired but Quinn. He scratched his nose and faced Declan. "Can I at least see the puppies first?"

Declan's eyebrows rose a fraction. "Uh, sure. Not a lot has changed since yesterday, though."

Quinn didn't care. When he woke up tomorrow, everything would be back to normal, so he wanted to make this last for as long as he could. Declan was more affectionate and close when he'd had a few, and Quinn fucking liked it. So what?

After agreeing that they'd come back and clean up tomorrow, the men said goodnight and split up. Alex and Kyle trekked to the staff house, and Declan and Quinn walked toward the cabins.

"It's cold in Alaska," Quinn mentioned. His teeth chattered a bit, and he noticed he hadn't zipped up his parka enough. "Is this really normal?"

"It's like two degrees—pretty average."

"Jesus." Quinn shuddered.

"Hold on." Declan halted them both and peered over at the fenced yard for the dogs. They could go in and out as they pleased, and several of them were outside right now, growling. Then Declan looked toward the airstrip and pointed. "Over there."

Quinn blinked and squinted. It was pretty cloudy, but the moon was bright enough to light up the snow that covered the airstrip. And he saw something. A few somethings, actually. *There.* Three, no, four. What the…?

"Wolves," Declan said quietly. "Beautiful, aren't they?"

"Oh, fuck that noise." Fear and adrenaline sobered Quinn in a goddamn second, and he hauled ass for the cabin.

Back home, Quinn wasn't a stranger to spiders and snakes—even the occasional gator—but Animal Control was only a phone call away. Wolves were a whole other matter. One, they couldn't be flushed down the toilet. Two, the nearest hospital was a plane ride away.

All roads supposedly led to Rome, and no roads led to Nowhere, Alaska.

"Are you coming?" he panted, tearing the door open. Thank fuck they never locked their doors in this state. He stomped his feet on the porch to shake the snow from his boots and looked incredulously at a chuckling Declan. "What is wrong with you?" Quinn threw out his arms. "Do you have a death wish?"

All casual and cool as a cucumber, Declan strolled over as if there weren't four bloodthirsty killing machines of the canine variety some hundred and fifty feet away.

"They won't come closer," Declan assured him, still too amused for Quinn's liking. "Not when we have a dozen dogs with their hackles up."

Quinn huffed and entered the cabin. "The dogs can't defend you. They're behind a six-foot-tall fence!"

"The wolves don't know that from over there," Declan pointed out, closing the door behind him. "You gotta relax, kid. It's important to be safe, but if you're gonna have a heart attack every time you encounter wildlife here, you won't last long. You could start by learning which animals to actually fear and not. Wolves attacking humans is almost unheard of, unless they're rabid."

Quinn stared at him flatly before he ignored to reply to Declan and took off his jacket and snow pants instead. Nothing he could say, anyway. Declan was probably right.

"How about I teach you to use a gun next week?" Declan suggested. "Can't hurt, you know. It'd protect you more than bear spray, too."

Quinn didn't know if he should be insulted. "Since when is Florida all about Disney and Daytona?" The Sawyer family had enough gun-totin' and tobacco-spittin' men to ensure everyone knew how to defend their bibles, bottles, and babes if it came to that. "You've *met* my uncles on Mom's side, Declan."

Declan blanched for a second. "Huh. You're right. So...if I let you borrow my shotgun, you wouldn't shoot off my foot?"

Moving farther into the cabin, Quinn spread a blanket over the made pullout couch and sat down. "There's nothing wrong with my aim, if that's what you're asking. So don't piss me off."

"Touché." Declan's mouth twisted up, and then he flicked his gaze at his bedroom. "Did you wanna see the pups, or...?"

Oh, right. That was why Quinn was here. Not because he'd grown addicted to Declan's presence.

CHAPTER 6

Declan needed Quinn to leave. Stat. They could check the pups, and then he could walk Quinn back to the staff house.

Preferably before Declan lost his fucking mind. The night had just been too much, and he'd seen too many, though equally perfect, versions of Quinn. Tipsy Quinn was up there with Swimmer Quinn, although Sore Loser Quinn and Candy Hoarder Quinn weren't far behind.

The kid had played poker, not to have fun, but to get his hands on as much chocolate as possible.

Declan wanted to fill Quinn's ass with his come for being so goddamn adorable.

Or see his release dribble down Quinn's chin…

Groan.

"Come on." Declan took the lead and opened the door to his bedroom. The faster he could get this over with, the sooner he could go to bed and stroke himself off.

He smiled a little when he found Lola stretching her legs outside the whelping box. Two pups were asleep, and the other three were looking for their momma's warmth. Which was a funny sight. Blind and deaf, they just tumbled around a bit.

"There's my girl." He squatted down next to Lola and scratched her behind the ears. "You miss the yard, don't you?" Living indoors wasn't for her.

She licked his scruffy cheek before she left him to drink some water.

"They're like little sausages," Quinn whispered.

Declan covered his laugh with a cough and pressed a fist to his mouth. Still on the floor, he peered up at Quinn, who appeared enamored of the pups.

He wasn't done whispering, either. "The cutest, weirdest, grayest, chubbiest little sausages. And I think I've picked my favorite. That one there." He pointed at…well, all of them. "The white one that has dirt or poop on him."

"Jesus Christ." Declan pressed his lips together to keep from laughing. "It's his coat, Quinn—copper and white. The father is gray and white, but that one will take after Lola." He thought about what he'd said and then carefully approached the pups. Lola watched but trusted him. And he gently lifted the pup. "My mistake. It's a little bitch."

"Don't be so fuckin' rude," Quinn hissed. "I know girl dogs are called bitches, but that doesn't mean I like it."

"Fair enough." Declan laughed quietly and stood up. "Let's go. I think you've offended Lola enough with the shit talk."

"Sorry, Lola." Quinn grinned and walked out, followed by Declan.

To his surprise, Quinn sat down on the pullout again, which meant Declan would have to *ask* him to leave.

"You wanna watch a movie?" Quinn asked.

No. I need you to get out before I maul you.

"Uh…" Declan checked his watch.

"Don't make me beg, Declan." Quinn offered a wobbly smile. "Firstly, I don't wanna die at the paws of the wolves that so rudely ruined my buzz. Secondly, I'm not tired. Thirdly, I-I…" He sighed and averted his eyes for only a second. "I like hanging out with you, okay?"

Declan didn't know what to say. He hadn't expected that much honesty, and now that he was facing it, he sort of gave up.

He wouldn't be able to deny Quinn *anything*.

He sensed how much Quinn had missed him every day while they worked, and it was incredibly humbling. It just wasn't in the same way Declan had missed Quinn. By the end of Quinn's stay in Alaska, Declan would be in shreds. That was becoming abundantly clear.

"Cable's out, but there's Netflix. I'll make popcorn." That was all Declan could come up with. And after popping a bag into the microwave, he returned to his bedroom to change in to sweats and a new T-shirt.

*

Quinn had stripped down to his thermals and switched on the small flat screen on the wall by the time Declan joined him with popcorn and two sodas. Before sitting down, he threw some more wood into the fire in the corner, and then Quinn could see his internal debate over where to sit.

With the couch turned into a bed, there was plenty of space, so if Declan was having problems, it had to mean Quinn needed to back down. He'd obviously made Declan uncomfortable.

"What do you wanna watch?" Quinn masked the feeling of rejection with a small smile and casually scooted up to one of the corners.

"I have a better question." Declan cocked his head. "Why are you sitting in the corner like a skittish animal?"

Was Quinn really gonna have to spell it out? Embarrassment colored his cheeks.

He shrugged as if he didn't care, when in reality he cared too much. "You looked like you thought I was hogging too much space."

Declan snorted and handed over the bowl and drinks. "Didn't know you could read minds now. But no, I was thinking where to keep the sodas. Maybe I should make a side table or something."

Relief flooded Quinn, and he solved their dilemma by shifting a little closer to the middle and then trapping his soda between the cushion and the armrest.

"Good enough." Declan sat down too and copied Quinn's move.

The popcorn bowl was the only thing in between them, and they settled for the classic *Psycho*.

"Lift." Declan fanned out his duvet and pulled it up until the bowl was in the way. So Quinn lifted the bowl, and Declan yanked up the duvet a bit more. "That's better. Let me know if it's not warm enough, though. We're expecting cold weather tomorrow. In Alaska, it could mean ten minutes ago."

"Cold weather? As opposed to what—the heat wave we're experiencing right now?" Quinn scooted down to a half-sitting position and got comfortable. He liked when Declan looked out for him, made sure he was warm and stuff like that. "How much colder could it get?"

"Oh, you have no idea." Declan smirked but didn't look away from the movie. "Let's just say that Alaska can turn antifreeze into her frigid bitch."

"Knew I was gay for a reason," Quinn joked back. "Less bitchy frigidness. Or frigid bitchiness."

He threw a handful of popcorn into his mouth and got engrossed in the movie he'd seen hundreds of times already. In fact, in various gaming communities online, he was well-known as BatesMadeMeDoIt.

Felt a little weird that he didn't even miss his gaming.

Was even weirder that he didn't feel the need to check in with his online buddies. For a long time, much of his life had transpired on the internet. If he wasn't working or spending time on the beach, he was attached to his laptop and headphones.

"Yeah," Declan said quietly after a while.

Quinn's brow furrowed as he wondered what it was in reply to, and he didn't get it.

Psycho sucked him back in. Time flew among knives and shower curtains at the Bates Motel, and when the movie was nearly over, Quinn looked over to see that Declan had fallen asleep.

Quinn silently brought the popcorn bowl and their sodas to the coffee table. Then he got comfortable again and pretended it wasn't intentional to end up closer to Declan.

There was nothing wrong with a little indulgence, was there?

Perhaps it was a creepy douche-bag move, but he wanted to "accidentally" fall asleep here. It would probably be the one and only time he got to share a bed with Declan, so fuck it. He was going for it.

He picked another movie at random and waited ten or fifteen minutes before he shifted closer so their legs touched.

"We should go to bed," he heard Declan mutter sleepily.

Fuuuck.

Quinn's heart raced, and he was pissed that his entire plan had gone to shit. He swallowed and tried to sound normal. "You think the wolves are still there?"

Yeah, that was lame. By the sound of Declan's tired chuckle, he thought so, too.

"Don't worry. I'm too tired to chaperone you." Declan straightened and yawned, stretching his arms above his head. "Lola will have to suffer with me. You can sleep out here."

There was no word in the English dictionary that could explain how much Quinn loathed that idea. He was all but crestfallen, which clued him in to the fact that this had gone way too far. He wasn't merely crushing on a straight man. He'd fucked himself over and developed feelings strong enough to depress him at the slightest loss of contact.

"I'll leave out a new toothbrush while I'm in the bathroom." Declan pushed down the duvet and got up from the bed. "I'll be quick."

Quinn wallowed in his misery alone for a few minutes. There was nothing he could do, though. He'd soak up everything until he went home at the end of March.

"Your turn," Declan said when he reemerged.

Quinn nodded in thanks and entered the bathroom, staring at his sad mug in the mirror while he brushed his teeth.

You are one pathetic motherfucker, Sawyer.

He rinsed and spat then wiped his mouth with a towel before he flipped off the mirror. The light switch was next, and then he opened the door, only to come face-to-face with Declan in the narrow hallway between the bathroom and the bedroom.

"I grabbed my pillows, but you can use my duvet. It's warmer." Declan pushed off from the doorframe and handed Quinn another pillow. "Is this okay?"

Quinn nodded and accepted it, unable to look him in the eye.

Of course, Declan had to fucking notice. "Are you all right?"

"Uh, yeah. Thank you for letting me stay." He managed a weak smile and then took a step toward the living room area. "Night." Before he could go farther, Declan took hold of his arm. Quinn stopped and frowned in question.

Declan raised a brow. "I'm not blind. Something's wrong."

Tell me about it. Quinn couldn't form a word. He *wanted* too much.

"Hey." Declan's voice softened, and he closed the distance to put a hand on Quinn's shoulder. "Whatever it is, you can talk to me. You know that, right? And if I don't know what's wrong, then how would I be able to fix it?"

That caused Quinn to let out a low, hollow laugh. "Thanks. I appreciate it—I really do—but this is nothing you can fix." He had already said too much, and now he averted his gaze for fear that Declan would see right through him.

Couldn't be too difficult.

*

There's no fucking way.

Those words went on a loop at a raging speed in Declan's head. And now...it was followed by a small "Is there?" that made him question every interaction they'd had.

He'd been awake when Quinn had moved intimately closer on the couch. He remembered the not-so-subtle touches during the poker game. The foot thing under the table. The glances. The request to stay longer. And when he now added the vulnerability in Quinn's expression, it seemed like everything had been handed to him on a silver platter.

In the small hallway, the tension crackled, and Declan couldn't believe it was only in his head. He wouldn't go so far as to claim perfect sanity when it came to Quinn, but this was too intense to be imaginary.

Declan had never met any of Quinn's boyfriends in the past, so he had no idea if the guy had a "type." It was almost incomprehensible to think Declan could be Quinn's type, yet if there was the slightest spark of hope, Declan would go for it. He *had* to. He had to know what it would be like, even though he'd have to be careful not to freak Quinn out.

One step brought Declan into Quinn's personal space. "Look at me." He slid his hands up Quinn's arms and shoulders to cup the back of his neck. At the same time, Quinn's wide eyes snapped up. *Fuck*, Declan's heart thundered in his ribcage. "Don't assume what I can and can't fix." With that, he pressed his body closer and lowered his mouth to Quinn's.

I need this to be what you want.

Quinn let out a noise laced with both need and surprise, and when his trembling hands grabbed on to Declan's hips, Declan's mind shut down. This *was* what Quinn wanted, which was all that mattered.

Lust surged forward. At the first taste of Quinn's tongue, Declan groaned and deepened the kiss. In a matter of seconds, they went from tentative and uncertain to hungry and aggressive. Declan slammed Quinn up against the wall, their tongues stroking and swirling. *Ease up, man. Be careful with him.* In return, Quinn let out a moan and shifted his hands down to palm Declan's ass.

"Jesus fuck." Declan growled, his cock growing hard and thick in his sweats. He could barely believe this was happening. Grabbing Quinn's jaw, he angled his mouth for a kiss he controlled completely.

Quinn was shaking like a fucking leaf, bringing out all Declan's possessiveness and protective instincts.

"Declan…" Quinn whimpered. "Are you sure you-you want—"

Declan cut him off before he could finish. "That I want this? That I want *you*?" He gave Quinn another deep, long, wet kiss and pressed their hard cocks together. "I've been sure for years."

Take it nice and slow.

"Oh my God." Quinn threw his arms around Declan and

kissed him harder, with more desperation. It was as if Quinn couldn't get close enough, fast enough.

Declan responded in kind, and they riled each other up with kisses and grabby hands for several minutes. Until Declan couldn't take it anymore. He wanted them in bed together—right now—so he started walking them to the pullout couch, his mouth never leaving Quinn's face.

"Let me take care of you." He kissed Quinn's jaw, neck, cheeks. He only paused to pull his T-shirt over his head, and then Quinn's, too.

"Anything you want—fuck," Quinn panted and fell down on the couch. "Wait." Before Declan could follow, Quinn gripped him by his hips and stared at Declan's erection. "Can I...?" He looked up.

Declan scrubbed his hands over his face, the sight of Quinn so close to his cock almost too much. "Like I'd say no."

Quinn swiftly yanked down Declan's sweats and then cursed and slowly brought his hand up. His eyes were glued to Declan's cock; he even licked his soft, thoroughly kissed lips, and Declan couldn't look away if he tried.

Without a word, Quinn wrapped his fingers around Declan before his mouth followed. There was a warm, openmouthed kiss first, and then a languid swirl of Quinn's tongue. A heartbeat later, as Quinn had half of Declan's cock in his mouth, his green eyes flashed open with the sexiest expression ever. Innocence mingled with greed, and Declan would've questioned his sexual experience if it weren't for that perfect fucking mouth that clearly knew what it was doing.

Declan was speechless and overcome with desire. It seemed Quinn wasn't much different, either. He closed his eyes and moaned around Declan's cock, sucking strongly and wetly.

It allowed Declan to give in to the pleasure completely, though he continued struggling against his need to take things further. His head lolled back, and he wove his fingers through Quinn's hair. *So fucking amazing.* Between the wet sounds and the feeling of sliding along Quinn's tongue, Declan's speechlessness was replaced with incoherent muttering and groaning.

His verbal filter got weaker.

"Perfect…goddamn perfect… Such a sweet mouth." He pushed forward and hit the back of Quinn's throat, and it constricted around the head. "Ah, *fuck*. That's it, suck my cock, Quinn. Suck all of me."

A hot flush spread across his face and chest, and he looked down through hooded eyes to see Quinn gripping his own cock in his thermals, stroking it rapidly.

"Don't even think about coming." Declan grunted and fisted Quinn's hair a little harder. His thrusts came faster now too, his climax approaching. As Quinn reached up to massage Declan's tight sac, he knew he was only seconds away from bursting. "Almost there." His voice was gritty and husky.

Quinn only redoubled his efforts, taking Declan's cock down his throat repeatedly and swallowing around the length.

Declan jerked back a few inches and lost it. The first rope of come coated Quinn's tongue. With a strained groan, Declan rocked deeper and rode out the rest of his orgasm.

When he came to, he wanted to fucking consume Quinn.

Nice and slow, he repeated internally. *Don't send him running.*

CHAPTER 7

It was still entirely dark out at ten the morning after as Quinn stood outside the cabin and let Lola do her business. She had huffed and head-butted Declan, who'd been closest, but it was Quinn who'd woken up, and he didn't want to disturb Declan. So Quinn had left the pullout couch, gotten dressed, and taken Lola outside.

All bundled up, Quinn sat down on the edge of the porch, his boots planted in the snow, and watched Lola sniff around the tree line of the forest across the road. Well, it was a road when it was shoveled. Now it was only a path and random tracks from snowmobiles.

Quinn's mind was elsewhere, though. He had a million questions about last night, yet he was completely serene and at ease. Too relaxed and warm, even out here in the cold. Perhaps because of the magic Declan had performed after Quinn had given him a blow job.

Never before had Quinn felt *worshiped*. He'd expected more kissing, a skilled hand, maybe even a mouth on him. That hadn't even been half of it. Declan had started out kissing Quinn, lying on top of him. Then his hands had begun wandering, and he'd quietly ordered Quinn to turn over.

Quinn shivered at the memory of the most erotic massage he'd ever received. With his spent cock resting in the crack of Quinn's ass, Declan had kissed and rubbed every inch of Quinn's back, shoulders, and neck. In less than ten minutes, he'd had Quinn panting and squirming.

Declan had moved lower to knead the backs of Quinn's thighs. Horny and beyond riled up, Quinn had buried his face into a pillow and spread his legs more, pleading for a release. Fucking *pleading.*

Instead, Declan had continued with his own agenda. He'd nuzzled Quinn's ass and parted his cheeks for a rim job with wet kisses, firm licks, and passionate tongue-fucking that had sent electric pulses of pleasure through Quinn.

"Fuck," Quinn muttered. Just thinking about it made him hard all over again, and he adjusted his cock as best he could in his snow pants.

He'd been harder than a fucking rock last night, and when he'd thought he couldn't take it any longer, Declan had told him to roll over a final time. And two minutes later, fingers buried deep in Quinn's ass, Declan had drawn an intense orgasm from him, swallowing every drop.

Quinn hadn't been able to move a muscle.

"Lola, you about done?" Quinn blew hot air into his gloved hands. "I'd like to grope your daddy a bit before we start our day." Then again, it was Sunday. What more did they have to do today? Quinn wouldn't mind staying in bed until tomorrow morning.

He also wanted more of Declan's dirty mouth. Jesus H, Quinn had nearly combusted when Declan had muttered about Quinn's "sweet mouth" during the blow job. Then when Declan had reciprocated—and then some—he'd been oddly quiet. No dirty talk.

Lola probably didn't have any fucks to give about Quinn's wish to head back inside, but she did want to return to her babies. She jumped through the snow until she reached the porch, only to shake it all off and send some flying straight in Quinn's face.

"Thanks." He grimaced and wiped his cheeks. "I'm feeling the love."

Once they were indoors again, Quinn toweled off Lola. Then she disappeared into the bedroom, and Quinn removed all his clothes.

Getting under the covers, he purposely slid his cold feet along Declan's calves and his less-than-warm hands over Declan's chest.

In response, Declan hissed and jerked back. "That's... That's fucking evil." He didn't sound mad, though.

Quinn smiled widely as Declan gathered him close and let his lips linger in a kiss to his forehead. Every now and then, there was a wince or a grunt of complaint when Quinn's feet made contact, but Declan never pushed him away.

"Thank you for taking Lola out," Declan mumbled sleepily. "You should've woken me up. Although, it was nice waking up to a beautiful man outside who wants to grope Lola's daddy." He cracked one eye open. "For the record, Lola's daddy wouldn't mind that at all."

Quinn rumbled a laugh, half embarrassed and more than halfway in love. "How thin are these damn walls?" He looked at the wall, only to see the window was open an inch. Having just been outside, Quinn figured that was why he hadn't noticed the slight nip in the air. "And I suppose you opened the window *before* you woke up?"

"Okay, I lied." Declan stretched his arms above his shoulders and placed one under his head. Quinn eyed the way Declan's bicep bulged a little. "I woke up when you closed the door behind you. The cold felt good, so I opened up a bit." Moving his other arm around Quinn's shoulders, Declan pressed his nose to Quinn's hair and hummed appreciatively. "You smell like snow, swimming pool, and come."

"*Jesus.*" Quinn coughed, his eyes widening. "Are you always this blunt?"

"Apparently. Sorry about that." Declan kept his eyes closed, and he spoke before Quinn could say that the last thing he wanted was apologies. Hell, he wanted more of that bluntness! It excited him. "I like the smell of snow. And swimming pool."

Quinn stifled a smirk. "And come?"

Declan let out another hum and shifted his lower body close so Quinn could feel his morning wood. "Yours? Love it."

This was surreal. Up until last night, Quinn hadn't even known Declan liked men, and now he was saying he loved the smell of Quinn's come. *What. The. Fuck.* Some light needed to be shed.

There was no way Quinn could forget Declan's comment last night, either. About not only being sure he wanted this, but he'd been sure for *years*.

"Hey." Quinn rolled over slightly so he was half draped across Declan's solid body. Quinn wanted to keep this comfortable, so he offered a dopey grin and said, "So that was pretty gay, what we did."

Declan chuckled gruffly and finally opened his eyes. "Get outta town," he deadpanned and then chuckled again. "You're too fucking cute sometimes." In a swift move, Declan was suddenly on top of Quinn, peering down at him with a lustful expression. "You know what I think?"

Quinn sucked in a breath and shook his head quickly.

"That I'm hungry," Declan murmured. After a quick peck on his lips, he kissed his way down Quinn's body and took his soft cock into his mouth.

"Fucking Christ," Quinn groaned and whipped away the covers. He was hard in no time, and the sight of Declan between his parted thighs was almost too much. *Almost.* He still wanted answers. "I gotta know what brought this on, Declan—*nnngh, fuck.*" Quinn threw an arm over his eyes and tried not to lose his mind.

"*You* gotta be more specific," Declan countered. He dipped low and began tonguing Quinn's balls. "Brought what on?"

"This," Quinn moaned. "All of this. You wanting me, you being into guys." He cursed again as Declan's fingers stroked him firmly. Quinn couldn't help but buck into his hand, wanting more.

He seriously wanted to get fucked.

"I've always liked women." Declan closed his lips around the head of Quinn's cock. Holy hell, what that man could do with his tongue. "Always loved men." *Liked. Loved.* Quinn registered what Declan was saying. "And I've wanted you since you were eighteen, nineteen." Declan sucked him in again, this time harder, and Quinn's hips pushed upward in reflex. *God.* "Want you even more now," Declan admitted.

Quinn was regretting starting this conversation while he was getting his dick sucked. More questions formed, but knowing that the attraction had been mutual for so long, combined with what Declan was doing right now, caused Quinn's brain to power down.

He stopped talking, and it wasn't long before he came down Declan's throat.

*

Declan was a man on a mission. He covered Quinn with his body, and the two made out like a couple of teenagers. Every time Quinn tried to take it further, Declan defused his advances and slowed down the kissing.

"Stop grabbing my cock," Declan chuckled breathlessly after a while. For the tenth time, he batted Quinn's hand away.

"I wanna suck you." Quinn grazed his teeth along Declan's scruffy jaw and squeezed his ass. "Are you really gonna make me beg for that? Not sure I'm that much of a bottom."

Declan wiped Quinn's smirk off with a deep, slow kiss. "I might actually make you beg, but not now. We need breakfast, and then I gotta check on the pups and talk to Sarah." A thought struck him, and he rose a little to gaze down at Quinn in question. "Out of curiosity, how much of a bottom are you?"

Quinn eye-fucked Declan's chest and gently raked his fingernails through the smattering of chest hair. "I prefer to bottom, no doubt, but sometimes I wanna top." He bit his lip, appearing to hesitate for a beat. "I can't really control myself when I'm in charge, though. I've been told I'm sort of aggressive and rough."

Well. Declan sure as fuck wanted to find out. He loved topping and wanted nothing more than to own Quinn's mind. The body came second. Declan liked to draw things out and hear pleas. He got off on tease and denial, and in his dreams he had Quinn writhing beneath him, begging to be stuffed, clinging to him, depending on him like a good little boy, and becoming mentally submissive in the heat of the moment.

None of that took force. In Declan's case, it took a nasty mind.

Though, being *taken* forcefully… Damn, he wanted that, too.

"You're getting harder," Quinn whispered. His hand snaked between them to fist Declan's cock. "Come on, I don't wanna leave the bed yet."

Obviously, Declan didn't want to leave the bed, either. He wanted them to remain tangled together for days, fuck hard until they crashed, make love passionately until they lost track of time, and draw endless orgasms from one another. But…he needed to clear his head, too. He was already living and breathing in a fog. Every thought, it seemed, was about Quinn.

It wasn't healthy.

Declan could already see himself taking care of Quinn, being there for him, controlling him at times to play out his fantasies, sharing his home with him, laughing at silly shit together, being equal in a genuine relationship… However, no one had ever wanted both sides of Declan. Additionally, Quinn was not only leaving, but Declan doubted they were compatible in every way. Hell, the kid had been stunned when Declan had noted the smell of sex. That was *nothing* in comparison to the stuff running around in Declan's head.

No, some distance was in order. Not enough for Quinn to get hurt, just hopefully enough to cushion the blow of Declan's imminent fall once he was alone again.

Yeah, yeah. Let's see how long this "distance" will last.

Declan ignored the sarcasm from within.

Last but not least, Lynn didn't have any right to be upset with Quinn. Quinn did have a right to be upset with Declan. And it probably wasn't smart to get too involved before he'd gathered the courage to tell Quinn about why he left Florida.

"Let me make you breakfast." He kissed Quinn and stroked his silky hair between his fingers. "We'll be back in bed before you know it." Another kiss, and he brushed his thumb down along Quinn's ear. His skin was so fucking soft and perfect.

"Buzzkill." Quinn frowned and pulled off a sad pout.

It only made Declan groan, and he left the couch before he could whip out his dick and smear pre-come all over that pout or something.

"I'll make you my pancakes." Declan stepped into his sweats and tied the drawstrings. Once in the little kitchenette nook, he still had a view of the front room, and he turned to see that Quinn hadn't left the bed. "What's up?"

Quinn was smiling, pushed up on one of his elbows. "I don't think anyone's ever made me breakfast." He scrunched his nose. "Unless you count my mom."

"Definitely not counting Pam," Declan replied, bringing out the ingredients. "What kind of relationships have you been in if you didn't make each other breakfast in bed at least once?"

Quinn shrugged a little and sat up, reaching for his boxer briefs. "Before I moved to Miami, sleepovers with boyfriends weren't exactly popular."

Declan cracked a few eggs into a bowl, nodding slowly. He knew Pam and Hank, Quinn's folks, had been supportive since Quinn came out at thirteen. Then they happened to live on the same street as a couple of Quinn's uncles and aunts who were only accepting because "God loves all his children."

There was never any talk of abandonment. Instead they wanted to *change* Quinn to fit into the Adam and Eve cookie-cutter mold, which meant whenever Quinn was seeing some boy, pamphlets for Christian summer school and boot camps that promised to cure homosexuality would appear in their mailbox.

Knowing Quinn's selfless ways and big heart, Declan was sure he'd kept things discreet while he remained in Sarasota—for his family's sake.

It had always angered Declan, and he'd been honest about it.

"What about when you moved in with Logan in Miami?" Declan wondered as he finished the batter. "He's always been on your side, hasn't he?"

"Oh, yes." Quinn walked over to the kitchenette and leaned his hip against the small counter. "But we share a one-bedroom apartment, and there's nothing private about having a bed in the corner of our living room, so…" He smiled faintly and folded his arms across his chest, averting his eyes. "Well, I suppose there'll be plenty of privacy when I go home. Logan's contracted to stay overseas a year."

Quinn's leaving was literally the last thing Declan wanted to think about.

And screw protecting himself. He was determined to spend the rest of their time together playing goddamn house, being the partner he wanted to be for Quinn—sans his deepest desires. Declan would just push those aside. He'd done it before.

"Let's not think about that." He left the butter sizzling in the pan and pulled Quinn close. "I wanna discuss your current living situation instead."

Distance, my ass. Couldn't handle five minutes.

"Oh?" Quinn fiddled with the drawstrings of Declan's sweats. "Wanna keep me around as your personal fucktoy?" He grinned.

Declan coughed and sputtered; *now who was being blunt?* Whereas Quinn cracked up at what was no doubt a joke, Declan killed his urge to say *"Yes, among many other things."*

"Jackass." Declan snorted and returned to the pancakes. "But yeah, I want you here." He snuck a glance at Quinn to gauge his reaction.

He was still grinning. "What, are you expecting me to say *no?* Give me a break."

CHAPTER 8

A few days later, it was clear to Quinn that he had to take the initiative when it came to sex. Sucking each other off and spending hours kissing under the covers was phenomenal, but Quinn was getting greedy.

He'd already broached the topic twice—well, to be fair, it was Declan who'd brought it up the first time. He'd been visibly angry with himself for forgetting… Blah, blah, blah, safety. It *was* important; Quinn didn't take it lightly, but Declan wasn't just anybody. Trust was involved, and Quinn couldn't imagine they'd do anything to put the other at risk. So after that first conversation, it was confirmed they were both clean and tested.

Quinn had been excited. He'd thought it was a prelude to Declan taking things further, and Quinn was sorely mistaken. So he'd asked frankly the day before yesterday. *Can you fuck me?*

How Declan had distracted him with his mouth instead was a fond, albeit fuzzy memory. But enough was enough. Quinn wanted to get ass-fucked before the week was over, so he was gonna cover all his bases. He worked hard by day to keep up with their schedule, and he made good on the lost bet and cleaned up after the pups as well as took care of Declan's kitchen duties. And now he was going to get his hands on condoms, in case Declan wanted that.

With a grunt, he hauled a large plastic trash bag onto the back of his snowmachine. All the bathtubs had been installed and tiled in now, so Quinn had spent the day clearing the bathrooms before Kyle and John got started on the toilets tomorrow morning.

"Hey, Quinn?" Alex hollered, emerging from the next cabin over. "Have you seen the boss man?"

Quinn nodded and gestured at the seventh cabin. "He's in Seven taking measurements for the kitchen cabinets."

"Thanks. Oh, hang on. You heading to the back?"

"Yeah." It was where they stored the trash, in a garbage shed behind the main house. "You need somethin'?"

"A new level if you can find one," he replied. "The liquid wasn't supposed to freeze, but…"

Uh-huh. "Welcome to Alaska," Quinn repeated, having heard it too many times while they worked. There was always something that wasn't supposed to happen. *But*, Alaska. "I'll see what I can find. Not sure I'll be back before lunch, though. Kyle will radio any minute."

That was why Quinn was getting ready right now. He wanted a minute alone with Kyle before everyone joined for lunch in the staff house.

"It's lunchtime already?" Alex looked surprised but happy. "Never mind, then. I'll wrap this up, and then I can find one after we've eaten."

Quinn nodded and straddled the snowmachine, starting the engine.

Disposing of the trash didn't take long, something Quinn counted as a blessing. The back of the main house faced nothing but forest, and that wasn't exactly reassuring when he was on his own.

It was very different up here from Nome, which was flat and almost completely bare. His two days there had only been the beginning of getting to know Alaska, and a new, odd little thrill tightened his gut at the prospect of sticking around a while longer.

If only he didn't have obligations back home. A thought that depressed him.

Quinn got back on the snowmobile and rounded the buildings, parking in front of the staff house. Smoke came out from the chimney, and with the kitchen window open a sliver, he could smell Kyle's huntsman stew.

Opening the door, he asked Kyle when lunch would be ready and began removing his parka.

"Five minutes," Kyle responded.

Good. That oughta be enough. Quinn entered the kitchen and ran a hand through his hair. "Smells good." Yeah, he wanted to be nice first. Give a little compliment before he asked for rubbers. "Need some help?"

Kyle side-eyed him as he checked the rice. "Cut the shit." He smirked. "*Suvat?*"

"What?" Quinn looked at him strangely.

"Ah. Sorry—force of habit. *Suvat* is slang for what's up," Kyle clarified.

"In what language?" Quinn had seen Kyle's tattoos, and some phrases were in a weird-looking language.

"Iñupiaq." Kyle added some herbs to the stew. "To you, that's Eskimo talk. Anyway, what did you want?"

Might as well just come out and say it, eh? "Condoms," Quinn said lamely. Kyle's eyebrows rose, and he stopped stirring. Quinn went on. "You've hit on me, you've hit on Sarah. John and Alex have wives at home. I thought if someone's got rubbers around here, it's you."

Now Kyle narrowed his eyes. "You didn't mention the boss, who we all know you're shacking up with."

"Yeah, funny story." Quinn cleared his throat. "Turns out he's my type."

"Didn't even know he was gay." Kyle turned to the stove once more, muttering something that sounded like, "That lucky son of a gun." Then he grunted and jerked his chin toward the stairs. "My room, nightstand drawer."

"Thank you, Kyle," Quinn said quickly, sincerely, and then turned for the stairs. "Really!" he called over his shoulder.

"Don't take all of them!" Kyle hollered back.

Hopefully, Quinn wouldn't need a single one. It was only to prevent Declan from using the lack of protection as an excuse.

*

Declan kicked off snow from his boots and then entered the staff house alongside Alex and John.

"Hey." Declan smiled when he saw Quinn was already seated at the table. Sliding in next to him, Declan gave his thigh a squeeze. "Everything good?" They usually worked together, except today Quinn had gone back and forth helping out where it was needed.

"Hell, yeah." Quinn smiled back and threaded their fingers together under the table. "Did I tell you I came up with a name for my puppy?"

His puppy. Declan loved it when Quinn called the pup his because it meant something permanent. He wouldn't stop caring about the little girl once he left.

"Lemme hear it," Declan replied as the others sat down.

"Where's Sarah?" John inquired.

"One of the dogs has an ear infection. She's tending to him," Declan answered. "She said she'll eat later." As he filled his plate, he tilted his head at Quinn, waiting for the name.

Quinn spoke in a quiet voice while he kept his eyes on the roll he was buttering. "Kieran. Although, I'll call her Kiery."

Alex frowned in confusion. "Isn't Kieran a guy's name?"

Yes.

Declan would know, what with it being his middle name and all. "It is." His chest felt odd. There was a warm, encompassing tightness, almost like a glove.

"Well, I like it." Quinn shrugged. "I prefer names with meaning, and what could be better than naming a pet after someone who means a lot to you?"

Christ. Declan set down his fork and took a deep breath. The glove-like sensation was still there, even stronger now.

"Someone from home?" Kyle asked, a crease between his brows.

"We met there, yeah." Quinn wore a funny smile. "So anyway.

Kiery it is."

Declan's hand returned under the table, and he grasped Quinn's with an affectionate squeeze.

With every day that went by, it was getting more difficult to separate fantasy from reality. Declan had even entertained the idea of asking Quinn to stay—to give them a real chance at something lasting. Then a minute later, Declan had remembered the secret he was keeping.

The longer he waited, the harder the fall…

He knew it was time to talk.

*

At the end of the day, Quinn was a horny mess. He'd even worked an extra hour after dinner to make sure Declan got to the cabin first to see the condoms.

Climbing off the snowmachine, Quinn began removing his beanie, gloves, and scarf before he even opened the door to the cabin.

"Hey." Quinn hung up his parka and ventured farther in. He was still in his utility pants and a hoodie, and he was in desperate need of a shower.

"Hey, yourself." Declan had already showered. His hair was damp, and he wouldn't be wearing his sweats and a T-shirt otherwise. "We need to talk once you're done in the bathroom."

Uh-oh. Quinn glanced at the pillows on the pullout and saw the condoms were gone. It had just been a joke, meant to be funny.

"That can't be good." Quinn studied Declan where he stood in the kitchenette, doing dishes. "Everything okay?"

Declan offered a forced smile over his shoulder. "That's not up to me."

That was actually reassuring. If it was up to Quinn, it meant things could stay the way they were. He doubted whatever Declan told him would be so bad.

"All right." Quinn snuck up for a quick kiss, and then he disappeared into the bathroom.

Despite the urgency to hear whatever Declan had to say,

Quinn didn't rush. He let the hot water loosen up the tension in his body. He no longer hurt the way he had in the beginning of this job, but a hard day's work still left him sore and tired.

It felt really good, though. He loved seeing their accomplishments, enjoyed the feeling of his body strengthening from the labor, and he slept easier at night.

Once he was finished, he toweled off, shaved, and slapped some aftershave onto his face. Next, he walked out with his towel wrapped around his hips. His hope was still to get laid, so he only changed in to a pair of boxer briefs. Then he joined Declan in the front room and sat down on the pullout.

Declan looked...withdrawn.

"Hey, whatever it is..." Quinn let the words hang there. How bad could it be?

It struck him that Declan might be ready to tell him what had happened in Sarasota six years ago, which formed a knot of nervousness in Quinn's gut.

"I saw the, uh, *treats* you left on the pillows." Declan sat down next to Quinn and pulled off a small, wry smirk. "Where'd you even find condoms?"

Quinn smirked back. "Kyle. In case you wanted to use protection, I wanted to make sure you had the option."

"Ah." Declan sat forward and leaned his elbows on his knees. "How thoughtful of you, I suppose." He huffed a small chuckle. "It's not about protection, though. The thing is..." He shifted slightly, and Quinn could see how uneasy the man was. Declan released a breath and scrubbed his hands over his face. "I didn't want us to go further before you knew the truth about why I left."

Quinn swallowed and remained outwardly calm.

Declan went on. "Your aunt has no reason to take anything out on you. It pisses me off to know how you were treated after I left, and I...I can't even tell you how sorry I am for not being there for you."

There was nothing Quinn could say, although he did scoot closer and squeeze Declan's thigh in silent support.

"I wasn't fair to Lynn during our relationship," Declan admitted. "I was up front—told her I didn't want anything serious—but once you and I became friends, I kept tagging along to family dinners so I could see you. Basically, I said one thing and did another, so the only thing I hold against her is how she treated you afterward." He shifted a few inches in Quinn's direction and faced him with an expression that screamed of both determination and shame. "First, I want you to know that a part of me thought you were way too young for me back then. Your age bothered me quite a bit, but whenever you and I saw each other, I didn't notice it as much."

"I was nineteen," Quinn protested. "We weren't even doing anything."

"I know, but that's just one part of it." Declan shook his head and looked over at the fire. "I have a...a fetish, I guess." He cleared his throat. In the meantime, Quinn was *very* interested to hear this. "Actually, that might be putting it strongly, but on occasion, I like it when—fuck. I like having my partner depend on me." His gaze slid back to Quinn's. "In bed. Kind of like innocence meets corruption."

"Okay..." Quinn wasn't sure he got it.

Declan could apparently tell. "Sometimes I want to take what I want when I want it, and the more vulnerable my partner is, the greedier I get. The sweeter my partner is, the dirtier I am."

That was...that was fucking hot.

Extremely hot.

And it slowly dawned on Quinn. What Declan was describing was a partner who was acting *younger*. "All right, let me see if I understand this," he said slowly, still processing. "You get turned on by someone who acts more innocently and younger."

"Sometimes, yes. *Acts* younger," he emphasized. "Not someone whose *real* age is close to jailbait."

Ouch. "Yeah, yeah, I get it. You thought I was too young." Quinn was a little annoyed. He didn't want Declan to see him like some kid. Not then, not now. "What I don't understand is why this is such a big deal. There's a whole fucking fetish community for this."

"I'm very aware," Declan replied dryly. "I've done my fair share of exploring, and that world is not for me. And it's beside the point. You were so easy to be around, but when I was alone, I struggled with guilt. I felt horrible for fantasizing about you in that way. You were my girlfriend's nephew, and I wanted to sneak away from family gatherings and go up to your room to feed you my cock."

"Jesus fucking Christ." Quinn lost the ability to breathe, and he flushed bright red.

He had to look away. He also had to put his foot up on his knee to hide his hardening dick.

Beneath the layer of primal lust though, he did see what Declan meant. At last. Quinn understood it couldn't have been easy to deal with. Basically, Declan wanted to play out his fantasies with someone who was mature enough to know what he wanted. He wanted to *play* the corruptor, not actually change—say a nineteen-year-old's—impressionable mind.

"I'm very sorry, Quinn."

Quinn didn't want him to say sorry. He just wanted to get this conversation over with so they could start screwing each others' brains out.

"Uh-huh, whatever. What does this have to do with my aunt?" Quinn asked. "As far as I know, she can't read minds, so she couldn't have known who you thought about—" The last word was barely out before he thought of something. "What, did you call out my name at the wrong time at the wrong place?" It was a joke. Mostly.

"*That* would've been less painful." Declan returned his elbows to his knees and looked down at the floor. "No, she showed up unannounced at my place one night. She had a key, so I didn't know she was there until she started screaming."

Sounds like Aunt Lynn, all right, Quinn thought. She always came and went like she owned the place. "Okay, so…" He felt the need to tread carefully here. "She caught you, I assume. Not with someone else though, right?" Quinn couldn't imagine Declan going so far as to cheat. "I still don't understand what it's got to do with me."

Declan chuckled quietly, completely without humor. "Oh, you were there—in a way." He sighed and never once looked up. "I'd printed out a photo of you."

"Oh," Quinn mouthed. He sat back, stunned. Flattered. Sliiightly amused. Which he definitely kept to himself. For whatever reason, Declan was seriously torn up about this, and laughing wouldn't help. Quinn could of course imagine tremendous embarrassment and even guilt, but shame? Not in the amount Declan still felt to this day, years later.

Hell, Quinn had jacked off to thoughts of Declan countless times, and he would've used pictures too, if he'd had any.

"I was actually asleep," Declan went on, scratching his eyebrow. "But it didn't take a genius to figure out I'd just gotten off. Gay porn running in the background, a photo of you in my hand, lotion and tissues on the nightstand—yeah, she was livid. Rightfully, of course. She felt betrayed."

Quinn agreed, *but*... "She also invaded your privacy. Had you told her she could use the key whenever?"

Declan shrugged with one shoulder. "Nah, it was for emergencies, but it was such a minor thing to even point out. Besides, you know how she is when she's angry. At one point, I was pretty sure only dogs could hear her. Or maybe I was just too busy dodging her claws."

"Okay, that's both comical and awful." Quinn shook his head. "So…what, she blames me for being the object of your desire? That's seriously fucked up."

"It was also the last direction I thought she'd take," Declan said. "Because after I'd grabbed her to stop her from—"

"What?" Quinn frowned. Had Aunt Lynn seriously resorted to that much violence?

"She wouldn't stop trying to bitch-slap me, and there's only so many times I can take that shit." Declan pinched the bridge of his nose. "Anyway, once I'd managed to calm her down, she changed her tune. She called me every name under the sun for the porn, and then—"

Quinn couldn't help but cut him off again, this time with a snort. "Come *on*. Everybody likes porn in one form or another. If they're not watching it, they're reading it. I get that she'd be upset with gay porn, but still." Jesus H.

"It wasn't just your average porn," Declan said in a voice that was practically dead. "Whatever, she actually painted you a victim. Which would've been totally understandable if she hadn't cut you out of her life and then turned your family against you."

It was too much to process at once. For now, Quinn filed away Declan's comment about the porn not being "average," and he asked, "How did she paint me as a victim?"

"She saw the photo," Declan replied quietly. "Her sweet, innocent nephew. Her sweet, innocent nephew who was a *child*."

I wasn't! Quinn wanted to scream. Fuck, he hadn't even been a virgin at nineteen.

This was ridiculous, and Declan wasn't done. "She was accusing me of wanting to take advantage of you. Every little thing I was conflicted about, she threw in my face." At last, Declan tilted his face enough to glance at Quinn. "I know the facts, Quinn. She did too, which is probably why she didn't make threats. But I've never been so ashamed in my life. I packed my shit and was gone before the sun was up."

Acting out of instinct, Quinn rose from the couch, only to nudge Declan back a little and straddle him. He hugged Declan, who was suddenly stiff as a stick. It only made Quinn hold him tighter.

"I'm sorry," Quinn whispered, and he really was. He was sorry that Declan had been through this alone. He was sorry for apologizing to Aunt Lynn when he'd never known what he'd done wrong. He was sorry for thinking that Declan had split just because he felt like it. Or as Aunt Lynn had told Quinn's mom one day when she'd been wondering, *"Oh, Declan? We're over. Good riddance, I say. He got a job out of state, and he's not worth following."*

Eventually, Declan let out a slow, heavy breath, and he started relaxing. He cautiously wrapped his arms around Quinn's middle, and he dropped his forehead to Quinn's shoulder.

"You don't hold any of this against me?" Declan asked, his voice barely audible.

"No way." Quinn tightened his grip further and kissed the side of Declan's head. Not only was there nothing to forgive, but Quinn's entire perspective had changed.

NORTHBOUND

He'd come to Alaska to get answers, to maybe fix the rift in his family, and now he was more concerned about Declan.

Somewhere along this short road, Declan had come to matter more than anything. Period.

CHAPTER 9

Declan moved silently around the cabin, pondering, tidying up, often glancing over at the sleeping Quinn.

He didn't know how long they'd held each other, and when Quinn had mentioned his legs cramping a bit, they'd only lain down and remained close. No talking. Just small touches, soft kisses, and affectionate squeezes.

Declan felt tons lighter. Nervousness lingered because of his preferences when it came to sex, but he had more faith in Quinn now. Less doubt in himself too, perhaps.

He couldn't sleep, though. He was at ease and tired, yet not sleepy. Instead he was rejuvenated. Like his slate had been wiped clean. Like he could look forward more rather than dwell on the past.

Around four in the morning, he took Lola for a walk. A cold front had rolled in during the night, and unless they got the cabins heated up, it would be too frigid to stain and finish the floors. There were still a million other things they could do, but taking the morning off and starting later held a big appeal.

Lola growled a few feet away, and Declan turned to see she had her teeth bared in the direction of the woods. He tilted his head, curious. The cabin was closer than the forest, and he carried a short-range firearm at all times, so he wasn't worried.

"Stay," he commanded Lola quietly. There was some rustling in the trees, and soon enough a black bear emerged along the tree line. It was a male, Declan noted, and it was thin. Most bears went into hibernation, though coastal Alaska was mild enough for some to stay awake through the winter. This one had been roused though, so it was probably testy as fuck and searching for food. "Come on, girl." Declan patted his thigh and turned, calmly walking back to the cabin. He looked over his shoulder every now and then, but the bear didn't come closer. "Lola."

Lola huffed and obeyed.

Come spring, they'd see bears almost every day, before the bear population thinned and the animals spread out all over the Preserve.

Quinn wouldn't be here for that.

Declan sighed to himself and closed the door behind him. He'd do his best not to think about the future, so for now…once he'd given Lola more food and water, he grabbed what he needed and stripped down to join Quinn in bed.

"*Christ*, you're cold!" Quinn groaned.

Ahhh, payback.

Declan wanted to take Quinn to Interior Alaska. Then he'd know what real cold was. Or maybe Kyle could tell the sunshine kid about the Arctic, where the permafrost made it difficult to lay pipes underground and regular batteries were useless.

"Get that sweet Florida ass over here," Declan murmured, pulling Quinn closer. "We'll be warm in no time."

"I *was* warm until you showed up," Quinn grumbled. Even so, he didn't have any issues snuggling up against Declan's body. "It's not time to get up yet, is it?"

Declan shook his head no and started dropping kisses along Quinn's shoulder. "We have a few hours." And he wanted to see how far he could go with Quinn.

"Does that mean I can quiz you about the porn you watched that supposedly wasn't average?" Quinn stretched, a sleepy grin in his voice, and pushed his naked ass against Declan's crotch.

Declan hummed and trailed his hand down Quinn's front to find him half hard. "Nothing much to quiz about." When Quinn shivered and exposed his neck, Declan planted an openmouthed kiss near his Adam's apple. "It was a man restraining a younger guy. Spanking him. Fucking him. Coming on him. Making him beg for cock."

"Fuck." Quinn swallowed.

Desire and relief flared up in Declan. Quinn's cock was hard in no time, allowing Declan to continue on the same path. *So far, so good.*

Releasing Quinn's erection, Declan reached up to brush some hair away from Quinn's forehead. "Would you let me do that, Quinn? If I told you lie down over my lap, would you let me finger-fuck you? Spank you? Hold you down and make you suck me off?"

Quinn shuddered violently then nodded quickly. "*Yes.* Holy fuck, yes."

"Good to know." Declan resumed caressing and stroking Quinn's body, exciting him further. "Very good to know." But that wasn't what he had in mind for right now.

Next to his pillow, Declan found the lube he'd gotten from his bedroom, along with a cock ring he sometimes used when he jerked off. The ring was made out of silicone, so he'd rolled it onto Quinn's cock before the guy could even see it.

"What—"

"Unless you don't enjoy what I'm doing, you don't have to speak." Declan pushed away the covers. "Just let me play with you."

Quinn mouthed an "Oh my fucking God" but remained silent.

Declan would never let himself be rushed, least of all with Quinn. With slow, firm strokes, he brought Quinn to the edge of orgasm with his hand, though he always stopped before it was too late.

Then he focused on stealing Quinn's breath with deep, passionate kisses. Stealing his own breath in return. Kissing Quinn was fucking glorious, and he kept doing it while he slicked up his fingers with lube and brought them to Quinn's ass.

"Finally," Quinn moaned.

Declan grinned as he slowly stretched Quinn's ass with his fingers. "You sound like you've been dying to get my cock inside you."

Quinn nodded and tried to face Declan more, and that was a no-go. Right now, Declan wanted Quinn's back to his chest.

When he deemed Quinn ready, Declan lubed up his cock and peered down between them. The blunt head pressed against Quinn's slick opening, and with agonizingly small thrusts, he eventually pierced through the tight ring of muscle. Declan stared, transfixed. He pulled out and saw the hole contracting again. Then back inside, only a couple inches.

"Don't tease me," Quinn groaned pleadingly.

"Spread your cheeks a bit," Declan said quietly. A wave of heat pressed the surface of his skin. "You have the sweetest fucking ass." As he pulled out yet again, he pressed down his thumb firmly at the base of his cock, causing a string of pre-come to trickle out.

He rubbed it over Quinn's hand that parted his cheeks.

"I wanna taste," Quinn panted.

"Maybe later." Without warning, Declan pushed in all the way.

A ball of pleasure exploded for a quick second, only for the sensation to tighten into a little knot again and settle in his gut. It would build up from there until he couldn't take it anymore.

"Fuck!"

"Shhh, baby." Declan stilled and moved his hand to cup Quinn's jaw. "Want me to pull out?"

"No!" Quinn pushed against Declan instead, and he tried to reach back to hold him in place. He twisted his arm a little and settled a hand on Declan's ass. "God, it feels so good. I want more."

"Soon." Truth be told, Declan needed a moment. Being inside Quinn was indescribable, and it'd been ages since he was intimate with anyone. Three years, in fact. And this wasn't a quick getaway to Anchorage, nor was it an emotionless fuck in a bar's bathroom with a woman who smelled like alcohol and cigarettes.

"You drive me crazy." Quinn angled his face back and kissed Declan's chin. "I should be used to it. You've been doing it since I was eighteen."

Declan's eyes flashed to Quinn. "Really?" He hadn't given it that much thought, but he'd figured it was new. Quinn had never once appeared to be attracted to Declan in Florida.

"Really," Quinn confirmed. "Now kiss me and fuck me."

Despite the surge of happiness, Declan wouldn't let the control slip through his fingers. "Did you just give me an order?" He lifted a brow.

To his satisfaction, Quinn bit down on his lip, clearly unsure of what to say in order to get his way. Declan smiled and smoothed out the crease between Quinn's eyebrows.

"Are you willing to say just about anything for me to fuck you right now?" Declan ground his cock deeper into Quinn's ass.

Quinn moaned. "Pretty much. I haven't been able to stop thinkin' about it."

Declan brushed a finger over Quinn's bottom lip, offered a sympathetic smile, and began to move slowly. "You're that desperate, huh?"

"For you." Quinn was exposed, need and vulnerability shining through. "Your cock. And Jesus, that mouth of yours. I can't help it."

When Quinn got to the point where he was begging, Declan couldn't hold back anymore. He withdrew his cock and rolled Quinn over so he was on his back. Declan followed and wrapped Quinn's legs around his hips before he slammed home.

Quinn threw his head back, his six-pack and pecs rippling as he tensed up. At the same time, his heels dug into Declan's ass, and Declan sank deeper into Quinn.

"I can feel you." Declan's voice was all sex. He pushed in and out of Quinn in long strokes and dipped down to kiss Quinn's neck. "Greedy little ass you've got. Every time I pull out, I feel you clenching down on me."

Quinn trembled, his eyes closed, and blindly searched for Declan's mouth. To Declan, it looked like Quinn was lost. Almost delirious. Mumbling pleas, labored breaths…

Declan's pace didn't falter. Like he'd said before, force wasn't his game. He kept every thrust deep and measured, loving the slow and steady climb of driving his man crazy with lust.

"I'll soak you." Declan peered down between them and saw his cock sliding in and out of Quinn's slick hole. "I'll fill you with my come. Will that satisfy you?"

"Yeah," Quinn whimpered. He lifted his head and latched his mouth onto Declan's shoulder. "Fuck—please. I wanna feel it in me."

"You will, baby boy." Declan let out a groan. Immense pleasure mingled with the sting of Quinn's blunt nails digging into his back. "You'll definitely feel it. And you'll keep it there until I'm ready to take you again." He imagined waking Quinn up in an hour or so, sliding into his perfect ass, and seeing come being pushed out with each thrust. "I want you dripping of me."

"Oh my *God*…" Quinn gasped and then moaned hoarsely and began writhing desperately beneath Declan. "Please." He met every push, and the urgency grew when Declan drizzled some lube into his hand and stroked Quinn's hard dick firmly. The cock ring had done its job, so Declan rolled it off and threw it somewhere next to them. He knew Quinn's release would be even more powerful now. "Oh fuck, please, please, please, please."

Those pleas went on repeat in quick, breathless succession as Declan sped up. "*Please, please, please, please.*" Declan's insides coiled up, his climax building up rapidly. "Please, Declan. Please, please." With a brutal kiss, Declan ground his cock deep inside Quinn.

"Wanna come for me, baby?" Declan swallowed before letting out a pent-up breath. "Ready to make a mess?"

Quinn never answered. As soon as the last words had left Declan's mouth, Quinn stiffened and went completely still. His lips parted, though no sound escaped. Eyes screwed shut. And then ropes of come splashed onto their chests, pulsing out of Quinn's cock.

The sight and the warm stickiness caused Declan to come undone. A strained groan slipped through his lips, and then he was drowning in ecstasy and emptying himself in Quinn for the first time that night.

CHAPTER 10

"What you're doing is highly distractin'." Quinn was on kitchen duty, but it was difficult to focus on the soup he was stirring on the stove when Declan was behind him, kissing his neck, being the owner of a pair of wandering hands. "Sweetheart, I'm fucking serious." Quinn chuckled and struggled not to give in. Which was nearly impossible with the hand cupping his junk. "You have work to do, and I gotta finish lunch before my mom calls."

He liked to check in with his folks once or twice a week, and tomorrow was Quinn's dad's birthday. So he was gonna discuss the gift with Mom around noon, half an hour before everyone came for lunch.

Declan hummed into the crook of Quinn's neck. "Speaking of tomorrow…"

Yeah, as if Quinn hadn't already thought of it. His dad's birthday happened to fall on Valentine's day.

"You wanna romance me?" Quinn asked with a smile. He added the frozen onion slices to the soup, followed by the diced potatoes. "We could always spend the day the way we've spent every day for the past few weeks."

Time really did fly when you were having fun. Or when you

were in love, Quinn supposed. He was halfway through his stay in Alaska, and with every night he spent with Declan—regardless if they were watching movies or having sex—Quinn woke up the next morning wishing time could slow down.

"Give me some credit," Declan replied with a soft laugh. "I definitely have plans for us."

Quinn couldn't wait. It would be the first Valentine's he spent with a boyfriend—if that was what Declan was. They weren't exactly hiding, merely remaining discreet. And Quinn knew it was because of a certain departure date. For as long as they didn't advertize their relationship, no one would ask the inevitable. *"What are your plans for after Quinn leaves?"*

Lately, Quinn had been thinking about what he had at home. Things he would miss if he left Florida permanently. Things he'd be happy to be rid of. But it always boiled down to obligations. He *couldn't* leave Florida at this moment.

"I have a gift for you," Quinn murmured, bringing himself out of those thoughts. "But I won't give it to you unless you let me finish lunch without you groping my dick."

Declan grinned into the kiss he dropped on Quinn's shoulder before stepping away. "All right. No need to make threats. I'll go check on the pups before I get back to John."

"Give Kiery a treat for me," Quinn said.

The puppies were a month old now, so they were running around the cabin, cute as *fuck*, and no longer looking like sausages. Quinn melted every time he saw the little shits.

Declan snorted. "You can spoil her on your own time. I refuse to take part in favoritism."

Quinn only gave Declan a look. As if Declan wasn't favoring Lola over the other dogs?

Ignoring Quinn's expression, Declan stole a quick kiss and then left the kitchen.

*

The reception was spotty at best, though Quinn usually found a good connection in his old room on the second floor. Seated on the bed, he filled his mom in on the progress with the cabins, told her he'd seen a huge moose the other day, gagged at Kyle skinning a caribou, and chuckled his way through a story about one puppy stumbling headfirst into the water bowl.

"Those rascals sound like a bowlful," Mom quipped before giggling.

Quinn laughed and picked at a loose thread in his thermal pants, trapping his phone between his shoulder and cheek. "You could say that. They get away with pretty much everything right now 'cause they're so damn cute. It's probably a good thing they're moving out to the other dogs in a month. They grow so fast, and it's like, whenever you turn around in the cabin, there's a puppy."

His mom chuckled before she stopped sort of abruptly. "Wait. So they live in Declan's cabin? I thought they were in the staff house."

"No, Declan's cabin is right next to the kennel. Plus, Lola's got him wrapped around her...well, paw, I guess. So when she was due, Declan moved her into his place."

There was a hum on the other side of the line. "Honey, just how much time do you spend in Declan's cabin?"

Well, shit.

There hadn't been a whole lot Quinn could tell his folks about the cause of the rift in the Sawyer family. It would've embarrassed Declan one way or another, and Quinn didn't want that. So he had—with Declan's permission—admitted that Declan had left because Aunt Lynn had found out he was into men, and she hadn't taken it well. Homosexuality and bisexuality were sensitive subjects among the Sawyers, to say the least.

Merely skirting around that topic ensured that Mom and Dad wouldn't confront Aunt Lynn. When they'd found out, they had just cursed her and said they were done trying to make nice.

Quinn didn't know what to say now. He certainly hadn't told them about the relationship. Because like Sarah and maybe even Alex or Kyle, Quinn's parents would without a doubt have questions about the future.

"Quinn?" Mom said carefully. "You're not developin' a crush on Declan, are you?"

Quinn winced. *Too late, Mom.* He was head over heels. "Um…"

"Oh, sweetie." His mom sighed. "It might be a good thing you're comin' home in a few weeks." She paused. "I'm not supposed to tell you this, but someone here sure is impatient for you to get back."

That made Quinn frown. Sure, there were a few family members he still got along great with, mainly his grandparents and two second cousins on his dad's side, but that couldn't be it. And he didn't have any friends left in Sarasota.

"Who?" he had to ask.

Mom hesitated for a beat before she whispered into the phone. "Logan."

"That makes no sense. He's in the desert somewhere in Iraq," Quinn answered frankly. "He'll be gone for a year, Mom."

"He had to come home," she said, and Quinn could tell something was troubling her. "Something happened. He's fine, but he was forced to break his contract."

Knowing Logan, it must've been serious. That worried Quinn. "Is he in Sarasota or Miami?" Logan's relationship with his own parents was frosty, but they did see each other around holidays. Otherwise, Logan actually preferred Quinn's folks.

"Miami for the moment," Mom said softly. "Not sure how long that can last, though."

That was it. Quinn couldn't take more of the vague crap. "Okay, we'll have to discuss Dad's gift later, Mom. I gotta call Logan."

After saying their goodbyes, Quinn plugged in his charger and called Logan's cell. And his best friend, who was usually carefree, picked up the phone sounding like he hadn't slept in a year.

"Quinn?"

"Yeah," Quinn said. "Is everything okay?"

There was a long pause before Logan chuckled tiredly. Wryly. "Lemme guess, you spoke to Pam."

"Don't tell her secrets." Quinn checked his watch, noting the others would be here for lunch any minute. "So, what's up? Why are you home?"

NORTHBOUND

*

The last hour of the day dragged by painfully slowly. Declan was itching to go home to his cabin and talk to Quinn. Because something was clearly wrong, and the only words he'd gotten from Quinn were *"I'll tell you later."*

"You mind if I take off now, boss?" Kyle asked. "All the radiators are installed."

Declan looked away from the cupboards he was staining and inclined his head. "Go for it. You have some big game in mind?"

Born and raised in Barrow, all the way up in the North Slope, hunting was more than a sport to Kyle. It was a way of life. Had it been anyone else, Declan would've been wary, but Kyle was a skilled hunter and survivor in the wild.

"Fingers crossed." Kyle packed up his equipment and zipped his parka. "I'll go load my sled, and hopefully I'll be back before dinner tomorrow."

Declan nodded. "Be safe."

"Where's the fun in that?" Kyle walked out of the cabin.

Left alone, Declan worked swiftly and thought about Kyle's last comment. The man was cocky, no doubt, except he'd calmed down the past two or three weeks. He no longer hit on Quinn or Sarah, and Declan had seen glimpses of loneliness in Kyle. The guy had also become guarded. Maybe it was easier to notice now when Declan wasn't so fucking lonely himself.

Kyle had traveled almost as much as Declan had, although Kyle hadn't lived outside of Alaska. Within the state, he'd probably lived in most boroughs in his thirty-two years. Yet, he always returned up to Barrow where his father and niece lived.

"At-fucking-last," Declan muttered to himself, done for today. He would resume work here first thing in the morning, so he didn't bother bringing his tools to the workshop behind the main house.

He switched off the work lamps and left the cabin, walking briskly toward his own.

Once he reached the small porch, he saw Quinn through the window, sitting on the couch staring into space. *Fuck the shower for now*, Declan thought. Whatever it was that bothered Quinn, Declan was gonna do his best to fix it.

He entered the warm cabin and took off his parka, boots, and utility pants. "Start talking, baby," he told Quinn, adjusting his thermal pants and rolling up the sleeves of his flannel shirt.

"Hello to you, too." Quinn gave a small smile.

Declan sat down next to him on the couch that hadn't been their bed in a week now. It felt good to share the bedroom instead, and the pups had more room to run around out here, anyway.

"I'm worried." He shifted on the couch to face Quinn more and covered his hand with his own. "Talk to me."

Quinn nudged Declan back a bit so he could rest his head on Declan's shoulder.

"I talked to Logan earlier," he mumbled. "He's home already."

"Okay?" Declan was confused. "Wasn't he gonna work overseas for a year?"

"Yeah." Quinn released a breath. "But that was before an ex-girlfriend dumped a doorstep bundle at his parents' house."

"Holy…" *Fuck*. Declan was shocked.

Quinn lifted his head and frowned at nothing. "Justin. He's two years old."

"Jesus Christ." Declan didn't know what to say. At all.

"Logan had no idea. For two fucking years, the guy had no idea he's a dad." Quinn looked like he was still waiting for the news to sink in. "His folks helped out for as long it took for Logan to get his ass home again, but they've backed out now. So Logan's alone in our apartment in Miami with a toddler and a shitload of paperwork."

Declan shook his head, feeling incredibly sorry for a young man he'd only met a handful times. Then selfish worries took over, and a cold rock of dread settled in his gut. *Was Quinn leaving early?* It would only take a phone call to order a bush plane up here. Mitch or his son would probably be able to make it within a day or two.

It was too soon. Declan wasn't ready. He'd never be ready.

"Where's the mother in all this?" he asked quietly.

"In Miami," Quinn answered. "Melissa, the ex, claims motherhood isn't for her, and she plans on bailing as soon as all papers are signed. She's dirt poor but lawyered up enough for this. She refuses to see the kid. Or Logan, for that matter."

"Damn." Declan scrubbed his hands over his face and tried to come up with any kind of solution that would help. "Have they established he's the dad?"

Quinn bobbed his head in a nod. "Now they're just working on custody shit."

Declan stared into the open fire, picturing Logan and what he was going through. "I can't even imagine—hell, poor guy." He sighed heavily and placed a hand on Quinn's leg, his chest constricting. "I'm gonna be honest with you, Quinn. I don't want you to go, but I would understand it completely if you wanna be there for him. I know you told me Logan took you in when you wanted out of Sarasota. He's your best friend."

Quinn dipped his chin and looked at his lap. "I did offer to fly home sooner," he admitted. "Logan insisted I stay. My mom's gonna drive down and be there for him until Melissa's signed everything. Then my folks will probably demand Logan stays with them for a bit."

It was too soon to be relieved, so Declan draped an arm around Quinn and kissed the side of his head. "It's up to you, baby. Like I said, I want nothing more than for you to stick around, but I don't want you to be miserable here. If you're worried about him…" He left the rest of the sentence unsaid. Quinn would understand without those words.

"I'm sure." Quinn linked their fingers together and brushed his lips to Declan's knuckles. Then he leaned forward and picked up one of the pups that ran over. "I'll probably check in with him every day, but he promised to tell me if he needs me to come home."

The tension in Declan loosened a bit, though it was temporary. In only a month and a half, it was time to say goodbye—unless one of them made a drastic life change.

Could Declan imagine going back to Florida? He'd never really liked living there.

He absolutely *loved* Alaska; this was home, but…he did love Quinn more.

"This is so fucked." Quinn's head lolled back, and he closed his eyes. The pup climbed on him, eager to play. His little tail wagged. "As far as I know, Logan didn't even want kids. We always said we'd raise hell by teaching my nieces and nephews shit and then return the kids to their parents."

Declan chuckled quietly as the pup jumped over to him instead. "Not a fan of children?" He'd always thought Pat and Nina would have a couple, though they appeared to love the wilderness more than starting a family in Nome. Which suited Declan just fine. He'd always preferred animals and less responsibility.

"No, I love them," Quinn replied pensively. "Just not for myself, I think. Maybe I'm too selfish. I don't know."

"You're the least selfish person I know," Declan murmured. "What about Logan? Has he changed his mind about children after Justin? When did all this happen, anyway?"

"About two weeks ago or something." Quinn yawned. "And he's definitely changed his mind. We didn't talk for that long, but I could tell he was hooked. He's scared out of his mind and cautious of course, but he's already protective of the little boy."

Declan hummed and said nothing else. He pressed his lips to Quinn's hair, inhaling the scent of the shampoo they shared. The light brown locks were unruly from his shower and still sun-streaked from twenty-five years in Florida. His tan had faded slightly, though it was barely noticeable.

Declan found the winters nice there, though the other seasons could go straight to hell. It was so goddamn humid, and while Floridians used and abused air conditioning, he'd rarely been comfortable there. He preferred the cold. Snow, crisp air, open fires, the lights on a clear night, and all smells that came with winter.

As for Florida… The beaches were beautiful. The man he loved lived there. Cuban food was delicious. Same with Mexican. Not dressing in layers and worrying about your car not starting was a relief.

"What do you miss from back home?" Declan didn't know why the fuck he'd asked that. Perhaps he was feeling masochistic. Or maybe he was trying to figure out if this could ever work. If

Quinn loved Florida as much as Declan loved Alaska...would they ever be able to feel at home?

Love came first for Declan, but he would never be comfortable if Quinn didn't love their home. And knowing Quinn's selflessness, he most likely wouldn't be comfortable asking Declan to move to Florida for him.

"The heat," Quinn said sleepily, snuggling closer to Declan. Wanting to accommodate him better, Declan let the pup down on the floor again, and he ran back to Lola by the fire. "More daylight. Swimming. Going out running along the beach in only board shorts." He paused. Declan's heart sank. "Logan and my parents, too. Oh, and fresh vegetables."

There wasn't a whole lot for Declan to say to that. In June, they had up to twenty-two hours of daylight every day, and aside from these three dead months every year, of course they had fresh produce, as well. Even so, Alaska wasn't Florida. Going out running here in only shorts...impossible in the winter, and in the summer there were the mosquitoes. Black swarms of them. Screw cologne. The smell of mosquito repellent beat everything else.

CHAPTER 11

In the first week of March, Quinn noticed a difference in Declan's behavior. It started the day they finished the bigger projects in the cabins. The kitchens had been installed, same with the bathrooms. Heating had been taken care of. The floors were finished. Small spotlights had been installed into the wooden ceilings, and they had divided all the furniture that needed to be assembled for each cabin.

Declan and John would be focusing on woodworking—creating bed frames, coffee tables, and nightstands—while Quinn, Kyle, and Alex would put together the rest of the furniture which had been ordered or made before the winter.

Perhaps it was the signaling they were almost done that caused the change in Declan. He remained loving, so attentive, funny, a god in bed, a great conversationalist, and he always showed interest in whatever Quinn did and said. But there was a sense of desolation in his eyes. Wistfulness. Moments of silence where he'd stand by the window and stare into space, lost in thought.

Quinn probably saw it easily because he was feeling the exact same way. In less than three weeks, he was getting on a plane back to Nome. From there, to Anchorage. From there, to DC. From there, to Miami. Each leg of that journey would take Quinn farther away from Declan.

"Lookin' good, boss," Alex said.

Quinn drew his gaze away from the couch he was assembling and saw Declan walking in with a headboard.

They exchanged a smile as they always did when they saw each other, but Quinn's gut twisted at the void that had grown. There was a distance—proof that Quinn was losing him.

"Kyle says lunch is almost done," Declan told them. "I'm just gonna drop this off in the bedroom, and then we can take an hour."

Lunch passed. They got back to work. More furniture was put together. The sun lingered a few more minutes with each day. Quinn took a quick break to tend to the pups that were eating solid food now. Kiery yipped and licked his cheek. Quinn was losing his mind. He breathed in the little puppy he'd come to call his own. He stroked her soft fur.

When he stepped outside again, he inhaled deeply, the scent of snow and forest and ocean salt and open fires filling his lungs.

Sarah passed with five dogs, smiling and waving.

John was next, driving another headboard on his snowmachine.

The day was winding down.

Kyle announced he was gonna start dinner.

Quinn stood still on the porch of Declan's cabin and followed the thin sunray peeking through the trees in the forest and hit the snow. Like diamonds, the snow sparkled and glistened where the sun touched.

Maybe they'd see the Northern Lights tonight. He'd seen them several times now, and they always stole his breath. Whether it was a neon glow that clouded the sky or multicolored streaks that pierced through in wavy lines, Quinn understood why it was called a show.

With tension growing inside him, Quinn finished his work and then followed the others to the staff house. An aroma of herbs, mashed potatoes with extra butter, steamed vegetables, biscuits, and grilled salmon enveloped them in the kitchen. Never before had he eaten better food. Rich in taste, perfectly prepared… The men around him knew how to take care of themselves.

Kyle and John were discussing hunting. Alex and Declan talked about upcoming projects for the spring and summer.

Quinn felt removed from it all, and it tore him apart.

*

Declan took an extra long shower at the end of the day. Having spent hours sawing, sanding, carving, and polishing headboards, he'd been covered in a layer of sawdust when he'd joined Quinn at home in the cabin.

He'd hoped to shower together, except Quinn had beat him to it, and now he was chatting to Logan on his laptop in the front room.

He's going home soon.

Those words had taken up residence in Declan's head and refused to be forgotten.

After washing off the day and loosening the tightness between his shoulders, Declan stepped out of the shower. He opened the door to let the steam out, and the fog cleared from the mirror so he could shave.

He was doing the left side of his jaw when Quinn trailed in and planted his forehead to Declan's back.

"You okay, baby?" Declan tilted his face up to remove the scruff under his chin. He rinsed the razor under the water and returned it to his skin.

Quinn merely nodded, his hands tracing the towel around Declan's hips. Goose bumps rose wherever Quinn brushed his lips along Declan's shoulders and back. The ghosting kisses then turned into heated, openmouthed ones, and Declan had to focus extra hard with the razor. His cock thickened, with no intention of delaying whatever Quinn had in mind.

Only a few random spots of shaving cream remained when Quinn dropped to his knees behind Declan. Long, skilled fingers worked the towel until it fell to the floor.

"Someone's on a mission." Declan washed off, then wiped his face with a smaller towel. "Anything I can help you with?"

"No." Quinn palmed Declan's ass and kneaded the cheeks firmly, sensually, and leaned forward. The touches were enough for Declan to register a change in the atmosphere. Something new. Quinn wasn't begging to be stuffed. He was in charge.

That made Declan shiver.

Quinn had taken plenty of initiative, but aside from a blow job here and there that he controlled, Declan was in charge. Even on the rare occasions Quinn fucked Declan, Quinn stayed compliant. Always asking. *Can I please go faster?* Always obeying.

"Fuck." Declan exhaled and hung his head, feeling Quinn's soft lips and wet tongue against his flesh. His cheeks were spread, and he gripped the sink as Quinn's mouth covered his hole.

Quinn hummed. His strong hands massaged, rubbed, and caressed. His tongue…was goddamn magical. Altering between sucking and tongue-fucking, he made Declan's knees weaker. With every lick, kiss, and wet swipe inside his ass, Declan's cock grew harder and harder. The skin around his length was tight, and he reached down to squeeze the base and give it a slow stroke. Quinn didn't seem to like that.

He stood up, his breathing labored, and pressed his own erection against Declan's crack. "Bed. Now."

Declan cursed, lost in a lust-filled haze, and followed.

He remembered Quinn's trepidation when he'd told Declan he tended to be rough and aggressive the few times he'd topped.

Declan couldn't fucking wait.

He joined Quinn on the bed, and there was no question about what was going to happen. There was a bottle of lube on Quinn's nightstand, and he had already stripped off his clothes.

"Do you know how much I hate the distance between us?" Quinn asked, covering Declan's body with his own. "This week, it's been like it's already over."

Something cracked inside Declan. "Quinn—"

"No." Quinn shook his head, his gaze following his hand that trailed down Declan's chest. "We can talk later. Right now, I gotta fuck you." He kissed Declan, softly at first, though it grew heated fast.

While Quinn blindly reached for the lube, they kissed deeply and hungrily. Declan wrapped his hand around their cocks as best as he could and stroked them firmly. Quinn's hand joined soon, only it was slick with lube.

Forehead to forehead, they both looked down and saw their glistening erections sliding together, fisted by their hands.

"You're so incredible, Declan." Quinn released them and rubbed his cock down to Declan's ass. "Sexy body, the best heart, filthy fucking mouth, perfect…"

Declan shuddered and clenched his jaw as Quinn slowly pushed inside in one smooth thrust. He wanted to speak, return Quinn's words—and then some—but he couldn't. It was overwhelming to feel Quinn's cock inside him. Amazing in the most primal ways.

He soon learned that Quinn hadn't been lying. He *was* an aggressive top, and Declan loved the burn. It fueled him, made him want more, and turned his dick into steel.

"I gotta go harder," Quinn panted.

It wasn't a question as it usually was, though Declan noticed the desperation seeping through along with the need for the proverbial green light. And in a flash, Declan gave it to him, his dominance surging forward.

"It's okay, sweet boy. Fuck me. Fuck me as hard as you can."

Quinn moaned and slammed their mouths together in a bruising kiss. They nipped and sucked, tongues stroking, and grabbed on to each other tightly. Declan grunted, feeling like his insides were igniting.

"That's it," Declan gritted out. Christ, he wanted to see Quinn's cock forcing its way deeper and faster. "You like it when I'm all spread out for you?" Quinn nodded quickly in response, and Declan reached down to stroke his own cock, still smooth and wet with lube. "Fuck, you feel good." Understatement. He'd never been taken like this before. Ever. "Whenever you need this, I'm here. Okay?"

"Yeah…fuck, fuck…" Quinn sped up, his balls rubbing against Declan's ass and the mattress. Then he grabbed Declan's jaw and angled them for more kisses, sloppy, wet ones. Labored breaths were exchanged. "Can't control it... Oh my God... *Declan.*" The name left him in a whimper.

"Take it all, baby." Declan was already getting close. Sweat beaded across his chest, temples, and forehead. "Anything you want. Take it."

Quinn shifted and slid a hand beneath Declan, cupping one of his ass cheeks. He used it for leverage, grinding deep, his hips swiveling. He was mumbling something too; Declan couldn't make it out at first. But as Quinn's thrusts became irregular and jerky—signaling his climax was close—Declan heard it. One word leaving Quinn's perfect mouth in breathless little mumbles.

"*Mine, mine, mine, mine, mine...*"

Something erupted inside Declan. Tingles of intense pleasure coursed down his spine. His balls felt hot and tight, and his release rushed up his cock. With a hoarse groan, Declan arched into Quinn and came. His fucking toes curled. His thighs throbbed. His ass clenched.

"Oh, *fuck!*" Quinn rocked deeper and buried his face in the crook of Declan's neck.

Liquid heat spread inside Declan's ass, a sensation that caused another couple ropes of come to trickle down his cock. He squeezed the base and brushed the pad of his thumb over the slit, completely spent and indescribably sensitive all over.

Quinn had collapsed on top of him, and all that could be heard was his rapid breathing against Declan's neck. If Declan concentrated, he thought he could feel Quinn's heart beating close to his own.

*

Afterward, the two lay in silence under the covers. Quinn snuggled closer and rested his head on Declan's chest. In return, Declan kissed the top of his head and gently drew his fingers through Quinn's hair.

He shivered slightly at the feel.

Quinn wasn't sure what had come over him earlier. Actually,

he did know, but he didn't know the trigger. Or perhaps it was a combination of things.

"Did I hurt you?" he asked softly.

"Never." Declan gave him a squeeze and pulled Quinn's leg higher up Declan's thigh. "But if I walk funny tomorrow, don't laugh."

Despite himself, Quinn smiled sleepily. Then he kissed Declan's chest before lying down again.

Something had to give. They wanted each other too much to just let this be some…winter fling or whatever. Hell, Quinn could imagine the rest of his life with Declan. But where?

Could he really pack up and move to Alaska? It was so damn remote. Cold as fuck. Dark.

Of course, there were upsides. He'd fallen hard for the cozy feel of this place, the food they cooked together, the breathtaking nature, the dogs, and he'd made friends. Then, he feared cabin fever, and he knew Declan didn't love Florida.

"Do you like Anchorage?" Quinn asked quietly. He'd only spent one night there because he'd been advised not to schedule connecting flights the same day. Alaska's weather was too unreliable. But the town—the little he saw—was beautiful. Expansive mountains made up the background of the coastal city, and Quinn had snapped off a couple photos with his phone.

Declan let out a drowsy laugh, his fingers absently trailing up and down Quinn's arm. "There's an old joke that goes, 'The best thing about Anchorage is that it's close to Alaska.'"

"What?" Quinn chuckled, confused, and lifted his head. "It's Alaska's capital, for chrissakes."

Declan raised a brow. "First of all, that would be Juneau. Anchorage just happens to be largest. Second of all, Anchorage is both wonderful and awful."

"How so?" Quinn ignored the small flush of embarrassment. He'd really thought Anchorage was the capital.

"Awful because it's turned into an average American city with chain restaurants and the same stores on every corner. Wonderful because it's convenient in many ways—close to a lot—the wilderness is in the city's backyard, and you gotta love Costco."

Quinn snorted and grinned, and apparently Declan was serious about Costco. He went on to explain how expensive food was and that a trip to Costco was like an orgasm for every Alaskan wallet.

"You're fucking adorable sometimes," Quinn laughed. "Okay, what about Juneau? Or Fairbanks? That's a city too, right?"

Declan smiled curiously. "Why?"

Was Quinn ready to spell it out? He had to. They had to try to find a solution. He released a breath and lay his head on Declan's chest once more. It was just easier without eye contact for this.

Though, rather than explaining his question, he chose another direction. "Would you ever consider leaving Alaska?"

"Oh." Declan had to understand now. "Well…" He sighed, and for a moment, Quinn was sure he'd upset Declan. But the kiss to his forehead said otherwise. "It depends."

"On?" Quinn prodded.

"On whether or not the person I'm moving for hates it here."

Quinn mulled that over, deciding he both hated and liked the answer. Declan had been honest, which was important. Honest and realistic. And it had also revealed that Declan wasn't unreasonable; it wasn't his way or the highway. He'd be willing to make sacrifices, too.

"I don't want us to be over, baby," Declan whispered.

Quinn closed his eyes and held Declan a little tighter. "Me neither. I just don't know what to do."

He'd told Declan about the IT job he had lined up when he returned to Miami, and with Logan unemployed at the moment, they needed the money to pay for their apartment. A small child was involved now, too. Quinn couldn't bail on Logan—not after everything he'd done for Quinn.

"You wouldn't be happy in Miami," Quinn mumbled. He didn't particularly adore Miami, either. Though, it did beat living permanently in the middle of nowhere where the population was officially zero.

"I'm happy with you," Declan replied quietly.

Quinn had almost expected the answer, and he could say the same, except this wasn't a fairy tale. Somewhere along the road, it would be too much. It mattered where they ended up. It was *home* they were talking about. Everyone deserved to love the place they lived.

"Can we change the topic for now?" Quinn asked weakly.

It was giving him a headache, and his fucking heart hurt.

"Sure." Declan removed his arm from around Quinn and scooted down a bit so they could face each other properly. They both placed their elbows on the mattress and rested their heads in their hands. "Hmmm…topic change, topic change…" Declan tried to make light of things, for which Quinn was grateful. "Oh, I know. You never told me how you tracked me down."

Quinn blinked. He hadn't seen that coming, although it made sense for Declan to be curious.

"I didn't have much to go on," Quinn admitted. "I definitely couldn't ask if Aunt Lynn knew anything, so my mom volunteered to ask and be subtle about it. It wasn't a shock that Lynn didn't know shit, but she did know about your folks."

So did Quinn. Declan had told him when they first got to know each other. His mom's health had deteriorated at an early age, so his father had retired from the Navy. Quinn didn't remember specifics but knew that Declan's mom had died, and Lynn mentioning it had sparked the memory. Declan's mom was buried here in Alaska. So was his dad, who'd had a fatal heart attack just two years ago. He hadn't learned that part until Declan told him a few weeks ago.

"So once I remembered that your mom was buried here, I wondered if maybe you had moved closer to your father." Quinn scratched his eyebrow. "I also knew Patrick ran some kind of adventure business, but for some reason I'd gotten it wrong. I thought it was in Washington. Anyway, I searched for O'Connor in Alaska, and the Retreat popped up."

Declan nodded and looked down between them, appearing lost in thought. "When was this?"

"Just last fall," Quinn murmured. "I wrote you a hundred emails and never pressed send." He frowned to himself. "We were so close… I figured since you left without a word, it was on purpose. You wouldn't have replied, would you?"

Declan smiled sadly and leaned in to press their foreheads together. "I'm sorry." That was answer enough. "No, I wouldn't have. I would've chickened out. I would've read every word as many times as you say you wrote them, but I was extremely good at making myself miserable."

Quinn nodded with a dip of his chin. "I figured. So when I saw the ad for a handyman on the website, I went for it." And the rest was history.

"I'm glad you did," Declan whispered.

Me too, Quinn thought. Even if it led to heartbreak.

CHAPTER 12

The day before Quinn was to leave arrived too fast.

Despite that they'd never announced anything outright, everyone had an idea about him and Declan, so the last dinner the night before was awkward and full of forced conversation.

Alex asked why a handyman would go home to work in IT, causing Declan to give Quinn a little wink.

"Nothing wrong with being a jack of all trades." Kyle smirked wryly at Alex, and that was true. Quinn had learned Kyle dabbled in plenty of areas. Aside from being an electrician, he was also a subsistence hunter, a lineman, fisherman, and rescue worker.

Quinn picked at his food and answered Alex. "I took a few classes when I moved to Miami. Computers have always been easy for me. It's just a temporary gig, though. Filling in for someone who's going on maternity leave next week."

He didn't feel the need to tell them he wasn't really a handyman. The cabins stood ready, so why even go there?

"We have computers in Alaska," Kyle mentioned casually.

Yeah... Thing was, Quinn *could* picture himself moving to this state if he could live in a city. He did love it up here in the wilderness, just not permanently. He was antisocial by Miami standards, though here in the middle of nowhere, he was more like a social butterfly.

"Construction season is also coming up," John pointed out. "Plenty of work."

Quinn scrunched his nose. "Construction season?"

For some reason, they all chuckled.

Sarah went on to explain. "There are two seasons here. Winter and construction season. It's like three months out of the year where it's warm enough to fix potholes and build houses."

Quinn grinned and looked down at his food. For the first time, it was tasteless.

His bags were packed in Declan's cabin.

I can visit. Declan can visit Florida. And how long could that last? Thousands of miles stood between them. It would be the motherfucker of long-distance relationships.

Quinn wanted more than that, and he only wanted it with Declan.

"So, are you excited to see your brother tomorrow?" Quinn tried to make conversation.

"Excited is a strong word." Declan smiled faintly. "It'll be nice to show him the cabins, though."

Quinn, John, and Alex wouldn't be here for that. Patrick and Nina would get off the plane, and Quinn would get on it with the cousins. They'd have enough time to chitchat for a few minutes before the pilot—Mitch, or whatever his name was—took off with three men, two of whom were eager to get home to their wives and kids in Anchorage.

Anchorage. Why couldn't Declan live there instead?

"Don't worry, guys. I'll be happy to claim all the credit," Kyle joked.

"You're a comedian." Alex clapped Kyle on his back.

Quinn tilted his head. "How long are you sticking around?" He'd only heard that Kyle had been asked to do some wiring in the main house.

"Couple more weeks." Kyle shrugged. "Then it's back to Barrow."

Another uncomfortable silence blanketed the kitchen.

That night, Declan spent hours making love to Quinn. They comforted each other with empty talk of daily phone calls and visits. Not that Declan didn't believe in the reassurances, but it wasn't what they wanted.

They collapsed out of sheer exhaustion around five in the morning, only to be awoken by the alarm a few hours later.

While they showered, Declan had half a mind to book a fucking ticket to Florida. While they got dressed, he wanted to suggest they live in both states. Six months in Florida, six in Alaska. Then he did the math and knew they'd never be able to afford to fly back and forth like that. The distance was just too great. It wasn't a quick journey.

Noon came around, and Quinn was sitting on the floor with Kiery.

Declan wanted to say he loved Quinn. He'd wanted to say it for weeks, but it felt like it would do more harm than good.

"I'll miss you, baby girl," Quinn whispered, kissing Kiery's soft fur. "I'll come back, though. As soon as I can."

When? Declan wanted to ask.

The sound of a plane's engine caused both men to look at each other.

This was it.

Quinn rose from the floor and eyed his luggage. Then he glanced at Declan again.

Declan closed the distance and pulled Quinn in for a tight hug. "I'll move with you," he blurted out. His own heart froze. But fuck it, he couldn't give up.

Quinn stiffened, though only for a second. He let out a soft breath and kissed Declan's neck. "No, you won't, sweetheart." He eased back and looked Declan in the eye, tears welling up. "I gotta think. Okay? We both do."

Declan didn't trust his voice, so he nodded once and cupped Quinn's cheeks, kissing him hard.

The flight down to Nome was almost as nightmarish as it had been on the way north, and the flight to Anchorage was only marginally better.

It didn't help that John and Alex were chuckling at Quinn every time the plane jerked, sank, and bounced.

Quinn nearly kissed the ground when they landed.

He had a night to kill in the city before his flight to DC departed tomorrow morning, and he gratefully accepted a ride from John, whose wife was picking him and Alex up.

John planted a fierce kiss on his wife's mouth and said, "Damn! I missed you, woman."

It was funny and sweet, and it also made Quinn's gut churn. He hadn't even left Alaska yet, and he was already sick with how much he missed Declan.

Selfishly, Quinn wanted to head to a bar or something and talk to Alex about everything, but he'd already vented to Kyle this morning. The man had stopped by while Declan had fetched breakfast in the staff house, and Quinn had been surprised to get an apology from Kyle.

"Just wanted to say I'm sorry for coming on so strong."

Quinn had said it was water under the bridge, and then they'd talked for a bit before Declan had returned.

"You're more than welcome to come over for dinner," Alex said, draping an arm around Quinn's shoulders. "We'll drop you off at your hotel, and we can pick you up, too."

Like he'd said, selfishly Quinn wanted to talk more—just get all these fucking thoughts out—but he couldn't. Alex and John had been away from their families for three months.

He smiled and shook his head. "Thanks for the offer, but you shouldn't play host tonight. Be with your wife and kids."

"Are you sure?" Alex eyed him skeptically. "My wife makes the best akutaq. You don't wanna miss it."

Quinn had learned akutaq was some kind of weird Eskimo ice cream, and he'd seen the chunky blueberry goo Kyle had made one day.

"Maybe next time," Quinn chuckled. "I think I'll just wander around the city for a bit."

That evening, Declan had Pat and Kyle over for drinks in his cabin. Declan was grasping at straws, so he ended up pacing and rambling for a good hour about everything, wanting help to find a way to fix this shit.

By the end of his verbal vomit, his brother and Kyle only stared at him. They looked a little shell-shocked. Perhaps because Declan had just used more words around Pat than he had the entire last year. And Kyle was bewildered because… Well, Declan wasn't sure.

"So, what do you think?" Declan looked expectantly at them, both seated on the couch. "Should I say fuck it and follow him to Miami?"

It didn't feel entirely right, but…

Kyle blinked. "Uh. Man, I'm the last one you should ask for advice. I've never been in a relationship." He rubbed the back of his neck and then shrugged. "So you love him?"

"Hold on." Pat leaned forward, fidgeting with the label on his beer. "You know Quinn from *before*?"

"Oh, yeah. That." Kyle snapped his fingers, nodding. "Answer that one first. I thought you met the guy when he came up here for work."

"*That's* what you wanna focus on?" Declan couldn't believe it. He grew frustrated as fuck, and his patience was wearing thin. "How about giving me a fucking hand and helping me instead?"

"Watch it, little brother." Pat smiled, though his cocked brow meant business. "I'm still processing everything—not to mention it's a shock to learn you're in love with a man."

Declan knew Pat was right about one thing; he needed to be patient. However, he rolled his eyes at the last comment. "You've known I preferred men since we were teenagers."

Pat nodded. "And the few times you've mentioned partners, they've been women. I mean, I don't care who you settle down with as long as you're happy, but it's still a surprise, all right?"

"Okay, I think I'm ready," Kyle said, facing Declan. "Real question now. How can you talk about moving to Miami when you won't even move to Anchorage?"

That made Declan frown in confusion. "What?"

"Quinn mentioned it." Kyle shrugged again and took a swig from his soda. "He said he'd asked you about Anchorage, and you didn't like it enough. And I'm with you there, buddy, but it'd be a hell of a lot better than Miami in my opinion. I'm never leaving this state."

Declan stared at Kyle as he tried to remember the conversation. He and Quinn had been in bed, and Declan recalled the joke he'd told about Anchorage being close to Alaska. *"It's both awful and wonderful,"* he'd said. Or something along those lines.

Had that been Quinn's attempt to compromise?

Declan felt like shit suddenly and irritated he hadn't picked up on that. He didn't want Quinn all the way down in Florida believing Declan couldn't be budged. Well, Quinn wasn't actually in Florida right now. He was still in Anchorage.

"Is this serious?" Pat asked. "You and Quinn, I mean. Would you leave this—your work, your cabin, everything you've got going here—for him?"

Declan would.

"You love this place," Pat pointed out. "And I gotta be honest with you, Dec. We need you here. Guests are arriving in a few weeks, and there's always something that needs fixing."

"I love him more," Declan replied, pinching the bridge of his nose. "I wouldn't ditch you guys here, though."

Quinn was right. They both needed to think.

*

Quinn was all but dead on his feet. With the flight time and time difference, he barely knew what day it was anymore. He'd known he wouldn't be able to catch the last flight to Miami, so he'd been forced to kill seven hours in DC, no sleep in sight and shitty food, and now he was on the first morning flight home.

He yawned and boarded the plane, stuffing his carry-on under his seat. Of course, he was sitting between a loud snorer who didn't know what personal space was and a woman who was yapping and gesturing wildly to her girlfriend in the row in front of them.

Pushing down his annoyance, Quinn located his headphones, found a playlist on his phone, and closed his eyes.

Again, sleep didn't find him. But at least it was smooth sailing—or flying—compared to the bush planes that were common in Alaska. And a couple hours and change later, he was back in Florida.

He followed the herd to baggage claim, and then his eyes got stuck on the exit signs. *Take me out of here.* He itched to fill his lungs with Florida air and feel the familiar warmth.

Unfortunately, this airport was the worst choice for that. The air was stifling, and the building was connected to the garage across the street, a concrete roof blocking the sun above.

He got in a cab and gave the driver his address, letting out a breath. *I know this place.* Latin music played on the radio. Palm trees lined the roads. The driver was on the phone, definitely not speaking English. Construction sites everywhere. Billboards in Spanish, ads for lawyers, heavy traffic.

Quinn was waiting for the tension in his shoulders to ease up, but by the time they were driving through Little Havana, he knew something was wrong. Too many things had changed. Not in Miami; with Quinn. *He* had changed. He just didn't know what, specifically.

When skyscrapers began filling the horizon, he texted his mom to say he was almost home and that he'd call once he'd gotten some sleep. She'd returned to Sarasota a couple days ago, having spent time helping Logan with his son.

Soon enough, Quinn was looking up at the building where he shared a small apartment with Logan. And Justin, Quinn supposed. That was weird.

He paid for the cab and hoisted up his bags, carrying them through the lobby toward the elevators. Three months of manual labor had strengthened every muscle in his body, so his exhaustion came from lack of sleep, not physical exertion. Although, his neck sure had suffered with the days of travel.

Reaching the fourteenth floor, Quinn got out his keys and heard peals of boyish laughter coming from his apartment.

It made Quinn smile. Logan was taking on fatherhood like a champ.

He unlocked the door and entered, spotting his best friend and his son on the couch in the small living room.

"Well, look who it is!" Logan deserted the couch as Quinn dropped his luggage in the entryway and closed the door. "Sorry we couldn't pick you up. I did the next best thing."

"What's that?" Quinn grinned tiredly, engulfed in a bear hug.

"We went out and bought lunch," Logan answered, and he didn't release Quinn yet. "I've also cleared out my bedroom. It's yours now."

"That's hardly necessary." Quinn patted him on the back. It was a little odd because Logan wasn't usually a hugger. "I've slept just fine in the living room." There was a bed in the corner that was his.

"Forget about it." At last, Logan ended the hug, and he smiled. A familiar smile—easy, carefree. Dimples hid behind his neatly trimmed beard. "Justin and I will stay in the living room now. You gotta have your privacy."

The only privacy Quinn cared about right this instant was being able to shut out the world so he could sleep.

"We can talk about that later," he told Logan. "For now, introduce me your kid. Then I'm crashing."

There were no snow pants or winter jacket to get rid of, so Quinn merely stepped out of his sneakers and walked farther into the apartment. He hadn't worn jeans in months, having been all set with thermals or utility pants, and it was a little weird. They weren't as soft.

"Baby, remember my buddy I told you about?" Logan squatted down in front of Justin on the couch.

Justin looked curiously at Quinn, who smiled politely and sat down on the couch.

"He looks like you, Logan." They had the same dark hair and brown eyes, and Quinn had seen plenty of photos of Logan was a toddler. Hell, a paternity test must've only been for the legal shit. "I'm Quinn. It's nice to meet you, kiddo." He grinned and ruffled Justin's soft locks.

Justin shrank into Logan's body but didn't appear scared. Maybe a little nervous. "Hi." He put his thumb into his mouth and snuck an arm around Logan's neck.

"He's cute, all right." Quinn smirked and turned to Logan. "Is it okay if we catch up later? I'm beyond beat."

"Of course, man." Logan nodded. "We're just hangin' out today. Cartoons and work applications are on the agenda."

Good thing Quinn already had a job lined up. Plus, he had three months of salary from Alaska.

They'd have to talk about that later, though. Quinn exchanged a few more words with Logan, and then he carried his bags into the bedroom. A dozen boxes with Logan's stuff were still there, but all Quinn saw was the bed.

Without even taking off his clothes, he face-planted on the mattress and pulled out his phone to send Declan a quick text.

I miss you. I made it back. Zzzz. Talk later.

As sleep took hold of him, he let out a long breath. A sense of relief finally hit him.

He was home.

CHAPTER 13

Declan spent the following week trying to get back to normal. He fixed things and made repairs where they were needed, the entire staff returned, Pat and Nina worked in the main house around the clock, Kyle helped out with blueprints for the new sauna they'd build this summer, and Declan visited the dogs a bit more than usual, his gaze always seeking out little Kiery.

Lola and the pups were with the rest of the pack now, and they were thriving, the pups growing every day, and Quinn wasn't here to see it.

Declan felt like he was being suffocated. For the first time, the Retreat didn't offer enough distractions. It was…emptier. And he felt incredibly removed from everything whenever he spoke to Quinn or got a text from him.

Even worse was when Declan's phone died because of shitty reception.

"You miss Daddy spoiling you, don't you?" He patted Kiery on the head through the fence. "I miss him, too."

"It's slightly worrying that you're talking to the dogs."

Declan smiled tightly and stood up to face Kyle. "Correct me if I'm wrong, but you talk plenty to Wolf."

Kyle had taken a liking to one of Lola's pups too, and would be taking it with him when he left after the weekend.

"I'm *training* him," Kyle insisted. "He's gonna be my hunting buddy when he grows up. There's a difference, boss."

"Whatever you say," Declan chuckled. "Did you want something, or are you just here to be a pain in my ass?"

Declan had half expected a dirty pun at that, so he was surprised when Kyle suddenly looked hesitant.

"Yeah...um, can we talk later tonight?"

Declan tilted his head, wondering what could cause that behavior. Kyle was always so sure of himself.

"Sure. You can always find me in my cabin with a bottle of whatever the fuck I can find." It was true. Since Quinn had left, Declan had been drinking way too much. It was only at night, but he wasn't usually much of a drinker, so he knew he had to quit it sooner rather than later.

*

Quinn hated his new job with a passion.

Sitting in a call center working as tech support and wearing a goddamn tie wasn't for him. He'd done it before, though not for some fancy corporation that insisted on a fucking dress code for the minions who were invisible. But it would pay the bills and allow Logan not to stress out and take the first job he could find. This week he was focusing on finding a good day care for his son, although he always had some applications to send out, too.

The buzz of scripted greetings and suggestions filled Quinn's brain. He adjusted the headset and took the next call, wishing he could be anywhere but here. Okay, not anywhere. The A/C was loud and chilled the workspace, yet the air remained heavy. Every breath made him want to return to the wilderness.

He hadn't appreciated the clear, crisp air in Alaska when he'd had the chance.

His phone vibrated in his pocket, and he pulled it out to see a text from Declan. A photo of Kiery was attached.

We miss you. Hope you're having a good day.

Quinn blinked against the sudden emotion that welled up. As he changed the picture to be the new background on his phone, he wished Declan could've been in the photo, too.

The relief that had struck Quinn his first day home was gone, and he feared it had been misplaced. He worried the feeling had been caused by the bed he'd desperately needed at the time and not necessarily by being back in Miami.

Returning to work, Quinn suffered through the sheer stupidity of some people, and the only thing that got him through the day was the plan of going out for dinner with Logan and Justin right afterward.

Just the elevator ride down after work was plain misery. He was crammed in the back, and everyone reeked of sweat, perfume, and sour moods.

And I'm coming back here tomorrow and every day after that for two months?

If it wasn't for the fact that Logan and Quinn would need more money soon, Quinn would've wondered why the fuck a mom needed two months off work after having a baby. Christ, dump the kid at the grandparents' house and get back to work, lady.

He'd really make a cool dad, wouldn't he? Obviously he knew he was wrong, which he blamed on this job. He groaned tiredly, exited the elevator, and tugged at his tie.

Logan and Justin were waiting outside, and the two-year-old waved happily as Quinn stepped out into the sun. *Scorching* sun.

"Hi!" Justin's favorite word, no doubt. That said, Quinn liked that the kid had warmed up to him fast. Even though Justin had been abandoned—literally—by his mother, he was a cheerful boy. He adored Logan.

"Hey, kiddo." Quinn squinted in the sun and wiped his forehead. "Is it just me or is it hot?"

Logan gave him an odd look. "Did your brain freeze in Alaska or something?"

Maybe. But it *was* awfully humid today, and it was only beginning of April.

"Whatever. Let's eat. I'm starving."

"And testy," Logan teased.

*

The weekend arrived, and Declan was still mulling over Kyle's offer. He had until tomorrow to make up his mind, and then Kyle was leaving.

For now though, the guy was here in Declan's cabin, and the two were watching a hockey game.

"I've missed TV," Kyle said.

Declan was indifferent about it. It saved money to only have internet here during the dead months, but everyone was back now, and so was the cable.

When Quinn had been here, they'd watched movies every now and then, but truth be told, neither of them was into much TV watching. More often than not, they'd forgotten whatever was on and had gotten lost in each other instead. Or they'd simply talked.

"You miss him a lot, eh?"

Declan nodded, keeping his eyes on the screen. He hadn't taken Kyle for being so observant.

"So what's keeping you from accepting my offer?" Kyle asked.

"It's not me," Declan admitted. "I want to, but it feels presumptuous."

"It'd also be one hell of a declaration. A grand gesture," Kyle pointed out. "Plus, I told you it's okay to back out. My friend will hook you up."

"Why are you even doing this, Kyle?" Declan turned to him, both curious and baffled. "You don't owe me anything. You know that, right?"

Kyle nodded and rubbed the back of his neck. "I don't know. I still feel bad for making Quinn uncomfortable. And you jealous." He smirked at that.

Declan huffed, though he sure as hell didn't deny it. "Watch the game, asshole."

*

Sunday rolled around, and Quinn wanted to hide out in his

bedroom. He'd spent Friday and Saturday with Logan and Justin, and Quinn was *tired*. He wanted to sleep, maybe Skype with Declan, and dodge calls from Mom. Instead, he was being conned into going to the beach.

Justin was a fucking witch. One dimpled smile and a well-placed "pwease," and Quinn couldn't say no.

They drove down to South Beach and bought food on the way; Logan also picked up a life vest, floaties, and toys for Justin.

"Are you excited, baby?" Logan looked back at Justin while Quinn drove their rusty car. It definitely didn't belong in South Beach.

"Yes!" Justin clapped his hands.

Logan chuckled and faced forward again. "Thanks for tagging along, by the way. I know you're exhausted."

"It's fine." Quinn smiled and slid down his shades from the top of his head. "I'll blame Justin if I sleep through my alarm tomorrow, though."

Logan grinned and squeezed Quinn's thigh. "Don't worry. I'll make sure you're at work on time. I can even play housewife and fix your lunch."

At that, Quinn barked out a laugh. Logan couldn't cook for shit, and everyone knew it.

After circling the neighborhood half a dozen times, they found a parking spot, and the three of them walked toward the beach. Justin's new board shorts matched Quinn's, which the kid got a kick out of.

"Looks like we beat the brunch crowd," Logan said. Quinn nodded, and they spread out their towels and sat down near the water. "Justin, come here so we can put these on." He was holding the life jacket and the floaties.

"But, Daddy…" Justin complained.

Quinn smirked at his buddy and left him to it, lying back and hoping to doze off. They'd applied sunscreen at home, and Quinn shifted as he tried to get comfortable, the sand sticking to his moisturized skin. Fuck, it was everywhere. And why was it so hot?

Maybe he should get in the water before he tried to nap.

Irritated, he sat up again and tore off his T-shirt. "I'm going in. Anyone going with?" He stood up and brushed sand off his shorts and calves. Between his goddamn fingers.

Logan said he'd stay by the edge of the water so Justin could play, leaving Quinn alone, which he didn't mind one bit. He waded out into the cold water and dove under, his body cooling down in an instant.

Better.

Justin was playing with his bucket as Quinn got back, and Logan's eyes never left his son.

"How long do you think it would take for Justin to reach the water?" Logan asked. "I'd be able to catch him, right?"

"Unclench, man." Quinn patted Logan's shoulder. "He's not even close, and you'd have to be stuck in a wheelchair before he could beat you."

Logan seemed to relax a little.

Taking a sip from his water, Quinn slid on his shades again and got comfortable. "Wake me up if I snore."

He did manage to catch a few z's, even though the sun was fucking blazing. Alaska was too cold and now Miami was too hot? When the hell could he find a happy medium?

Some time later, he roused when someone blocked the sun.

"You three make the cutest family!" a guy said.

Quinn didn't move, although he did open his eyes behind his shades to see Logan's reaction to that. Over the years, many had taken them for a couple, especially in South Beach—which was the capital gayborhood of the East Coast—and Logan had always just laughed it off.

Now he was smiling, however. "Thanks."

What in the actual fuck?

*

"This is the last day, Dec," Pat warned him. "Guests are arriving *tomorrow*."

Declan knew. He walked around the spacious condo once more and eyed it critically. It had a balcony with a spectacular mountain view, a big plus, but he wasn't sure about the size. Were two bedrooms necessary?

"It's big, isn't it?" Declan turned to his brother.

Pat shrugged and looked around. "It just looks that way 'cause the living room and kitchen are together." He tapped the counter with a solid wooden top that worked as a divider for the two areas.

Declan preferred it simple. For that reason, he could afford this on his own dime because he'd saved up most of his money from six years of working at the Retreat. The pay wasn't huge, but he didn't have rent or utilities or even food to worry about.

Anchorage was pricey as fuck, though. And unless two incomes would eventually support this, Declan couldn't keep it forever. Besides, he wasn't sure they needed a second bedroom.

"You like this place," Pat said firmly. "You barely looked at the other condos, and you've checked this one out for two hours now. You like it. You're just apprehensive. It's okay. Now, let's go sign some papers so we can get back to the Retreat before Nina tears me a new one. I told her two days, and it's been three."

"I'm not signing anything," Declan answered with a frown. "Not until Quinn has seen it."

That was the deal. Kyle's gracious offer. Declan could decide on a place, and then he had one week to let Kyle's Realtor friend know if he was gonna draw up the papers or not.

"Okay." Pat folded his arms across his chest. "So now what? Are you on the next flight to Florida?"

Declan became nervous thinking about it. That *was* the next step. Would Quinn accept it? Would he be happy here? Declan could definitely see himself living here with Quinn. What Declan had said about Anchorage was true, and that included the good things he'd mentioned.

He'd talked things over at length with Pat and Nina, and they had reached an understanding when it came to work. It wasn't optimal, but if Quinn agreed to move so far away for Declan, it was incredibly worth it.

Declan could travel back and forth, spend a few weeks at a time at the Retreat, and then return to Anchorage until they needed him again. He'd get a second job here, as well.

"I gotta buy the airline vouchers, too." Declan pulled out his phone to look up the airline that had the best flights between Alaska and Florida. As a gesture, he wanted the checks to let Quinn know they could visit Florida whenever he wanted. If Declan had to work extra hours, so be it.

"I'm pretty sure you can do that at the airport, little brother."

"Right." Declan should've thought about that. Fuck, he was nervous.

"Kinda cool to see you all in love and shit," Pat laughed quietly. "It's a good look on you."

Declan flipped him off but was unable to withhold his smile.

A lot was at stake and so much could go wrong, though he was ready to try now. He'd given this a lot of thought, and it all came down to being with Quinn. He had to. No ifs or buts. Declan would do his best to accommodate both of their wishes, and it was easier to do that when they were together—not a whole damn country apart. Three weeks had been too much, only proving Declan wanted it all—everything—with Quinn. Permanently.

"All right. I like this place." Declan nodded.

CHAPTER 14

Quinn had the apartment to himself for once on Thursday. Logan and Justin were hanging out with a single mom and her daughter, and Quinn hoped Logan got laid or at least got his dick sucked. Because the guy had been acting weird lately. In fact, he'd been different ever since Quinn got back to Miami almost three weeks ago.

He couldn't put a finger on what it was, but…it was almost as if Logan was trying to get closer. And that didn't make sense. Logan was straighter than an arrow.

Right?

Surely Logan would've told Quinn if that had changed.

Pushing those thoughts aside for now, Quinn flipped through the channels until he saw a polar bear. Of-fucking-course. A documentary about the Alaskan wilderness.

He moaned in complaint and lolled his head against the back of the couch. As if he wasn't already missing Declan enough? Jesus H, Quinn was struggling every single day. And not only about missing Declan but about constantly comparing Florida to Alaska.

They usually went out to eat at restaurants here; in Alaska it was mostly home-cooked meals. Glorious, rich in taste, home-cooked meals. The sand on the beach here felt nice between his toes, though he hated it elsewhere. In Alaska, could he even find beach sand?

The humidity was starting to bother him here, but was it worse than the cold in Alaska? He did miss the crisp air. And how the snow crunched and pressed together beneath his boots.

Driving a snowmachine was a hoot and a half. Bears freaked him the fuck out. The city noise and pollution in Miami gave him headaches nowadays. He kinda, maybe, sorta wanted to go on hikes and bring Lola and Kiery. And guns. 'Cause, Alaska.

Turning his focus to the documentary again, he got his answer about the beach. There was at least one in Alaska because he saw as the camera zoomed in on a large bear walking along a beach. Overcast sky, wind tearing through the bear's fur, rain spraying, waves crashing, sand getting stuck to its paws.

It was a Kodiak bear, Quinn learned, and wasn't that a fucking trip? Declan was born in Kodiak. The city with the same name as the island on which it was located.

Swiping up his phone next to him, he sent Declan a message.

Did you know that the Kodiak bear is the only bear that can compare to polar bears in size?

Declan replied fairly quickly. Perhaps he wasn't working.

I did know that. What I don't know is what you're doing quizzing me about bears all the way from Miami. Everything okay, baby?

"No, everything ain't okay," Quinn moped. By now, he'd learned more from the documentary, so he responded.

I'm watching a documentary about Alaska's wildlife. Did you know there are no ants on the island for Kodiak bears to eat?

He closed his eyes for a beat, imagining Declan taking him to visit the island he'd been born on. Quinn knew very little about it, except Declan had said you either loved it or hated it. Oh, and many residents there were somehow connected to the Coast Guard.

Imagining things with Declan…of course it led to more lewd thoughts. Quinn missed touching him, getting fucked by him, hearing what a "sweet boy" Quinn was for taking Declan's cock so perfectly…

"Damn," he whispered. His cock thickened, interested in this development.

He'd expected to jack himself raw without Declan there, but the opposite had happened. Quinn was down in the dumps, and he probably hadn't gotten off more than a handful times in the past three weeks.

He was hard as a rock now, though. If Declan had time, perhaps they could jerk off together on FaceTime. That would be fucking hot. So he opened his eyes again and saw a message was waiting for him.

I knew that, too. Did you know there are many beaches and golf courses in Sarasota?

That prick. Quinn chuckled and gave his cock a lazy stroke in his shorts. Okay, point taken. He'd stop quizzing Declan about the place he knew best. Rather than writing back something witty, Quinn pulled down his shorts to reveal his cock, and then he smirked and took a photo of it.

He sent the shot to Declan with the caption, ***Up yours.***

"Meh, not too shabby." Quinn thought it was pretty witty, anyway.

Not ten seconds passed before Declan called.

"Are you saving that for me, baby?"

Quinn hummed, getting more turned on just by hearing his man's voice. "Well, it definitely misses you." His eyes closed again, and he allowed himself to travel back to Declan's cabin. Quinn remembered the rich scent of the place. Campfire, furniture oil, snow, always some kind of food, soap, *sex*. "My ass misses you, too." He thought about taking out a vibrator or something, but he didn't know when Logan would be home, and frankly, he was feeling too lazy to get off the couch.

"You have no idea how much I miss—" Declan's voice was cut off by a mechanical-sounding ding, followed by an echoing voice that said something about unattended baggage.

That cleared the sex-filled fog Quinn was in, and he sat straight up. "Where are you?"

"Nome," Declan replied with a yawn. "Supply run—on my way back to the Retreat now."

Oh. Quinn sank back into the couch again, and he tried to push down his disappointment. The background buzz seemed like it belonged in a larger hub, but he was no doubt wrong. Wishful thinking could be a convincing bitch.

He'd certainly lost his erection, so he tucked his cock back into his shorts and sighed internally.

"I'm sorry," Declan went on. "Probably not the best place for phone sex."

"It's okay," Quinn said, though it wasn't. It really, really wasn't. He missed Declan so much it almost hurt. What the fuck was Quinn doing? He looked around himself at the apartment. Empty walls, furniture that didn't belong to him, and it didn't feel like home. Had it ever?

When Quinn thought about home, his mind traveled to that cabin. Risk of cabin fever or not, he had to get back, didn't he? Maybe he could persuade Declan to travel into larger towns every now and then.

Right?

Things couldn't go on like they were, that was for sure.

"I gotta board," Declan said softly. "You off to bed soon?"

"Yeah." If Quinn could sleep. "Text when you can and be safe."

After disconnecting the call, he stayed immobile for a long time while his mind was running a mile a minute. He rationalized about the weather, knowing it was all a matter of adjustment. If Miami was too hot for him, it only meant his body was still used to the cold in Alaska. The dislike for the humidity here would fade in a couple of weeks. He'd prefer the climate here. The same went for Alaska. If he moved there, he'd get used to it. It wouldn't always bother him, would it? He wasn't even sure it had bothered him in the last weeks leading up to his departure.

He couldn't ditch Logan without warning, but he could plan. He could talk things over with Logan and set a time.

Quinn would miss his folks, but when he thought about it…it wasn't like he saw them all the time. Even when living in the same state, they often went months between visits.

Perhaps he could find a job that allowed him to work from home—the cabin.

Quinn's pulse kicked up a notch.

Was he really doing this?

Fuck, yes.

Just as he stood up from the couch, keys wriggled in the door. It opened, and Logan walked in with a sleeping Justin in his arms. The kid was already in his PJs, so Quinn assumed Logan had gotten him ready for bed at the woman's house.

"Hey." Logan smiled warmly.

"Hey. How was the date?" Quinn stepped aside to give them room. Justin preferred to sleep on the couch, and Logan used Quinn's old bed in the corner. "Did ya get some?"

"It wasn't a date." Logan gave him a quizzical look. "I just want Justin to make friends."

Huh. Quinn raised his eyebrows and sat down on a stool by the kitchen bar. "Did the single mom know it wasn't a date?"

At that, Logan took on a sheepish expression. "There may have been a misunderstanding." He kissed Justin on the forehead and threw a sheet onto the couch before lowering his son to it. "What did you do tonight?"

Jacked off to Kodiak bears.

Okay, not really.

"Not much." Quinn absently drew his thumb across his bottom lip, thinking about going to bed. Or maybe he should talk about his plans now? "Talked to Declan a bit."

"Ah." Something tightened Logan's features. "You're a real sweetheart, Quinn—keeping in touch with your old hookups like that."

Quinn reeled back slightly, surprised by the edge in Logan's tone. "Excuse me?" He hadn't been completely truthful to Logan, who knew the entire past about Declan but not the details on how it had unfolded. Nor did Logan know exactly how serious Quinn and Declan had become in Alaska. It wasn't a fucking hookup. And even if it had been, Logan had way too much venom in his voice for Quinn's liking.

"All right, I'm sorry. That was uncalled for." Logan covered Justin with a light blanket before joining Quinn near the kitchen. "It's just…" Frustration and something akin to desperation flitted across Logan's face.

Quinn stood up to be face-to-face, and he was ready to defend himself if it came to that.

"It's just…" Logan struggled with his words, then wet his lips nervously. And before Quinn could react, Logan closed the distance and tried to kiss him.

In the last second, Quinn managed to turn his head so Logan got his jaw. "What the *fuck*, Logan?" Quinn couldn't have been more shocked. He stared wide-eyed at his friend, a guy he'd known over twenty years. A guy who'd always been *straight*.

Anger and confusion unfurled in Quinn, and he grabbed Logan's arm and dragged him into the bedroom so they wouldn't wake up Justin. Once the door was closed behind them, Quinn whipped around and widened his arms.

"Mind telling me what the hell is wrong with you?" he asked incredulously.

Logan winced and glared down at the floor, his jaw ticking with tension. "I would if I could. I'm…confused."

"Join the club." Quinn did his best to push down the anger because he wasn't sure Logan deserved that much of it. After all, the man didn't know Quinn and Declan were serious about each other. "Why did you kiss me, Logan?"

Logan didn't have any difficulty answering that, though he refused to look up. "Because you're leaving."

Quinn opened his mouth, only to close it again. "Wh-what?"

"You forget that I know you, Sawyer." Logan huffed and folded his arms across his chest. "You could never lie for shit, either. Didn't take a genius to see you're completely hung up on Declan." He cocked a brow at Quinn. "I saw it back when he lived in Sarasota, and I see it now."

Shit. Quinn ran a hand through his hair and chewed on his lip, processing. He thought he'd been fucking stealthy back in the day, keeping his crush on a straight man secret.

"You're moving up there, aren't you?" Logan spat out. "You

two hit it off more than you let on, and now you're leavin'. What the hell is it with Alaska?"

Quinn threw him an irritated look. "Ease up, for fuck's sake. If you're so sure about me and Declan, then why would you hit on me, huh? What kind of douche-bag move is that?"

That changed Logan's expression. He went from visibly upset to embarrassed. "I wasn't thinking clearly. I'm sorry about that." Sliding down along the door, he ended up on the floor with his hands tugging at his hair. "I'm happy for you. I'm just... I can't even begin to explain how exhausted I am. I don't know what the fuck I'm doing, Quinn." When he looked up, all Quinn saw was how completely lost Logan was. "You know what I did after your mom left here? I sobbed like a fucking child in the bathroom."

The lingering anger drained out of Quinn in a heartbeat, and he squatted down in front of Logan. "You should've told me." He knew that was hypocritical, but he didn't care. "You're a great dad to him."

"Doesn't feel like it. I don't feel like *myself* anymore."

Quinn suspected he didn't even know half of it. He couldn't imagine what it would be like to wake up one day and suddenly be in charge of another human being.

"You should take my folks up on their offer," he murmured. "They love you as much as they love me, Logan. You know that, and they want to be there for you."

Logan grimaced and rubbed his face tiredly. "Then I'd be on the same street as my parents. Seeing them for holidays is one thing, but if I lived there... Christ, they'd always find a moment to bitch at me for being a disappointment."

Ah, yeah. Logan's parents were special people. Both were doctors and had always wanted their only child to follow in their footsteps. When he'd instead gone into construction, they'd had a fit and had basically stopped caring about him.

"Leave that to my mom." Quinn put a hand on Logan's shoulder. "Seriously. Justin is the only grandchild she'll have. She wouldn't let your folks ruin that."

Logan groaned. "After what I did out there, please don't imply I'm your brother, Quinn."

That sure as hell relieved some of the tension, and Quinn grinned.

"Will you think about it, though?" he asked. "You already have a room there, and Mom would be thrilled to help with Justin while you get back in the game. What do we have here, anyway? It's been a great escape for both of us, when we needed it."

"You really are moving to Alaska, aren't you?" Logan smiled a small one.

Quinn nodded hesitantly. "Yeah. Not until you're on your feet, but... I love him."

Logan sighed. "I know you do. Can't believe I actually tried to kiss you."

"Yeah, about that." Quinn sat down properly and squinted. "Has something changed, or were you just afraid I'd leave?"

It took a long time before Logan answered. He seemed to be deep in thought, frowning. Then a small shrug. "I really don't know," he said quietly. "I guess...I guess I've had thoughts..." He blew out a breath and averted his eyes to the floor. "When you moved in, I wondered what it would be like."

Quinn was stunned. How had he never noticed? "And now?" he asked carefully.

"With *you* it would be too weird." Logan cracked half a grin, and Quinn was honestly relieved. The last thing he wanted was for things to get uncomfortable. "Fuck if I know, Quinn. I see a woman and I immediately check her rack. It's probably nothing." He got a little dismissive about it.

Quinn, for once, saw that Logan was downplaying something, but he didn't want to push.

"Well, I'm here if you ever wanna talk," he murmured. "Someway, somehow. I'm not ditching you. You know that, right? I mean, even if I'm in Alaska..."

"Yeah." Logan nodded. "Thanks, man."

"Anytime." Quinn meant it, too. "Hey, what do you say about acting a little rash tomorrow?"

Logan appeared intrigued. "What do you have in mind?"

"Sarasota." Quinn really believed Logan would feel better there, and unlike Quinn, he actually had friends left in their hometown. "My folks have been texting and calling nonstop since I got back. They wanna see me, and you could check things out. One weekend. Feel it out a bit."

"It's only Friday tomorrow," Logan pointed out. "You have work."

"Fuck it. I'll call in sick." Hell, Quinn had more than half a mind to quit altogether. He was suddenly aching to get out of Miami. "We can head out early and beat traffic. Have breakfast on the way and be in Sarasota before lunch."

Logan was mulling it over, Quinn could tell. He looked tempted as fuck, further proving Logan needed to get away as much as Quinn did.

"Our lease is about to expire," Logan said pensively.

That was how Quinn knew Logan was on board. Not only with the weekend, but later, too. Logan was ready to start over, and to Quinn's immense relief, he wouldn't be alone.

They wouldn't be renewing their lease this time.

Before Quinn went to bed that night, he fired off a quick text to Declan.

I have good news, I think. We're going to Sarasota tomorrow morning, but call me when you can. I love you.

It wasn't until hours later when he shot straight up, disoriented from sleep and panicked from reality, that he realized he'd just told Declan he loved him. For the first time. In a motherfucking text message.

His heart raced as he reached for his phone in the darkness. There was no response, and Quinn didn't know what to think about that. At least it gave him the opportunity to apologize.

Shit, shit, shit.

Sleep still had a grasp on his brain, but after four tries, he sent a message that didn't make him cringe too much.

I'm so sorry. I didn't mean to tell you that way. It just felt natural. I'm such an idiot. I do love you. I love you so much, but I wish I could've told you face to face.

Falling back against the mattress again, he stared up at the ceiling and cursed himself to the fiery pits of hell.

"I'm a fucking moron," he muttered.

CHAPTER 15

Declan grinned to himself as he reread the texts from Quinn. He'd received both when he'd gotten off the plane in New York, and he could see they'd been sent three hours apart.

Those three little words were powerful. Powerful enough to push past exhaustion and the moment of oh-fucking-hell-they're-not-even-in-Miami. There hadn't been a flight to Miami when Declan had needed one, so he'd booked one into nearby Fort Lauderdale instead. Going through baggage claim, he grabbed his one bag and then looked for the signs toward car rentals.

He called his brother on the way, and they were busy welcoming early arrivals at the Retreat. He also texted Kyle to fill him in and wish him good luck, because it was April and the whaling season had started. Kyle wasn't due to set sail with his niece's Native elders until tomorrow, but Declan didn't trust the cell service.

Kyle's response made Declan chuckle...then freeze in his tracks.

Thanks for waking me up in the middle of a hot dream. Because of that, I hope you run into your ex in Sarasota. Peace out!

"Goddammit," Declan muttered, entering the terminal for rentals. Considering the entire Sawyer family lived in the same neighborhood—several on the same street—it would be weird if Declan didn't run into at least a few of them. He could only pray he didn't have to see Lynn.

*

"Are you *still* freaked out?" Logan laughed. "He'll take it well, man. Chill."

Quinn pressed his lips together in a grim line, wishing he had the road or something to focus on. But Logan was driving, so... And yes, Quinn was still freaked out about the texts. Declan hadn't replied, and it was morning in Alaska. He'd be up by now, and he always checked his phone before starting his day.

"Daddy?" Justin asked from the backseat. "I'm hungwy."

"We're almost at Nana and Pop's house, baby," Logan said into the rearview. "They'll have lunch ready." He shot Quinn a brief glance. "Pam asked to be called Nana."

"Of course she did," Quinn said with an easy smile. "You're family, and she won't be getting any grandkids from me."

Logan seemed to relax in his seat, which confused Quinn. Logan should have gotten used to this by now.

"No kids for you and Declan, then?" Logan asked as he switched lanes. Their exit was coming up.

"Nah." Quinn was thankful his best friend was okay with things now. "If everything goes well, we'll have two dogs instead. I miss that little girl more than I thought was possible." He'd shown Logan a photo of Kiery, and he couldn't wait to see her again. "Is it wrong I want Declan all to myself? Besides, we'll have Justin to spoil when I finally convince you to come up and visit."

Logan chuckled. "Me in Alaska? That'll be the day."

Quinn was gonna make sure it happened. End of discussion.

The gates to his parents' neighborhood came into view, and they passed a small lake before entering the grounds. It was gonna be really nice to see his folks for a bit. Quinn had missed them, and he was particularly grateful for their close relationship right now.

"Ten bucks Mom is waiting in the driveway," he told Logan.

Logan hummed, thinking it over. "No. Since they retired last year, Hank's been enjoying golf during work hours. I think he's just gotten back from a round, and Pam is fussing over him."

Quinn disagreed, so they shook on it.

When they took the turn leading to their street, it looked like Logan would win. Mom wasn't there, but then she exited the house before she could've seen Logan and Quinn's car.

"Dude, I win." Quinn smirked.

"The fuck you do! She wasn't there from the beginnin'!"

"She came out before she saw us," Quinn pointed out.

Logan wouldn't back down, so in the end they said they'd find another bet. And by that point, they'd pulled in next to where Mom was beaming and clasping her hands under her chin.

"Took you boys long enough to get here!" she chided before throwing her arms around Quinn. "It's so good to have you home, honey. Let me see you." She stepped back and appraised him before smiling widely. "You built some muscles up there in Alaska." She hugged him again. "You're not Daddy's chicken-legs boy anymore, are you?"

Quinn grinned and kissed the top of her head. "When did he ever call me chicken legs?"

"When you weren't listenin'." Then she was done with Quinn because Logan had helped Justin out of the car, and the kid was the new star of the show. "Oh, there's my little boy!"

For being such a small lady, she had some strength in her. She engulfed both Logan and Justin in a hug and kissed their cheeks while she complained that she never saw them.

Didn't matter that she'd recently stayed in Miami while Logan signed the paperwork that drove his ex out of his life.

Quinn and Logan got left behind to carry in their luggage, and Mom kidnapped Justin to head inside. "Lunch by the pool in ten minutes," she called over her shoulder. "Don't forget to wash up!"

Logan scratched his eyebrow with the car key. "Have you been replaced, buddy?"

Quinn nodded and checked his phone. Fuck, still no response from Declan. He was getting anxious. "I wouldn't bet against it, that's for sure." And hours later, he knew very well he'd been replaced.

Mom and Dad listened with interest as Quinn told them about his three months in Alaska, and they had countless follow-up questions to each story, but Justin was always there. Either on Dad's lap or Mom's, he had their attention, too.

Quinn definitely didn't mind. He adored Justin a whole lot, and he liked seeing his parents being Nana and Pop.

During all this, it seemed they never stopped eating. First lunch, then iced tea and sweet rolls, then there was a fruit plate, then a taste-testing of cookies that Mom was bringing to her book club next week, and lastly it was time to get dinner ready.

Dad was busy. He gave Justin a kiddie set of brightly colored plastic golf clubs, so they stayed behind in the backyard with Logan.

Quinn wanted to break the news about Declan gently, so he followed his mom to the kitchen. On the way, he checked if there were any messages on his phone. There weren't.

Had he fucked it all up?

"I have to ask you somethin', honey," Mom said as she checked the chicken in the oven. "Are the golf courses any good in Alaska?"

What a strange question. "Um…" Quinn's brow furrowed, and he got started with the green beans. "I wouldn't know—I didn't see any. But I can't imagine them being better than here."

"Good. Then I don't have to worry about your daddy wantin' to go up there anytime soon." She turned to him after getting the rice out of a cupboard. "Did you see the way his face lit up when you mentioned the fishin'?"

Quinn had. He thought it was a good sign. Dad enjoyed going fishing every now and then, and it was a fisherman's dream to see Alaska.

"Would it be bad if he wanted to vacation there?" Quinn asked, testing the waters.

"Of course not. But you know how I feel about flyin'." She side-eyed Quinn. He could practically feel the stare. "So before I get down to business, I have to know about Logan. He brought more luggage than what's needed for a weekend. So did you."

"Is that a fact?" Quinn withheld his smile as he ran the green beans under water. "Maybe we did."

"Quinn Andrew Sawyer!" She found a spatula to whack him with.

"Ow!" Quinn hissed and rubbed his elbow. Jesus, his fucking *elbow*. There was no goddamn padding to protect him from abuse. "Hateful!" He threw her a scowl.

"You ain't seen nothin' yet, son." His mom put her hands on her hips and she cocked a brow. "Now stop teasin' me. Is Logan finally movin' in? I'd ask him myself, but I don't want my fragile heart broken again." She sniffled and averted her eyes for effect.

Quinn wanted to roll his eyes, except that would earn him another whack. "No wonder I'm gay. I was born to the most dramatic—" He wisely cut himself off when Mom reached for the spatula. "What I meant to say was… Yes, my sweet, wonderful mother, Logan is most likely moving in." Mom squealed in happiness, and Quinn went on. "He's gonna check in with some old friends and put feelers out for work. Our apartment's month-to-month, so don't expect him to move in today, but soon. Better?"

"So much," she gushed. "And I'm gonna want to kill you in a second, aren't I?"

"Whaa…?" Quinn's clever response reflected what was in his head. Mom was still smiling about Logan, though her eyes had taken on a wicked glint.

She nodded. "Time to get down to business. Are you leavin' your mama?" As she lifted a delicate brow at him, she traced the length of the spatula with a perfectly manicured fingernail. "Don't think I didn't notice how Declan was in every story about Alaska." Quinn swallowed nervously. "One can't help but wonder if that crush of yours was reciprocated. Plus, you said Logan's movin' here—not you. Yet, you're givin' up the apartment."

So much for breaking the news—or merely bringing up the idea—gently. His mom had already figured it out.

"Have you thought this through, honey?" Mom asked, her tone growing soft and concerned. "You're very different people."

Not that different, Quinn wanted to say. "I didn't even confirm he reciprocated."

Mom scoffed. Of all things. "Oh, please. How could he not want you? My girlfriends down at the club always say you're a hot piece of…*ass*." The last part was whispered, and Quinn let out an incredulous laugh. "You're a total sweetheart, too."

Quinn shook his head, amused, and happened to look out the kitchen window to see one of his uncles leaving something in the mailbox. Which could only mean one thing. The family on the street knew Quinn was in town, and the religious nuts wanted to be helpful and drop off the latest "How to Straighten that Gay Backbone" propaganda.

The crazy thing was, before Aunt Lynn had turned most family members against him, all these preaching people had always been sweet to him. They loved him in their own fucked-up way and never avoided him, yet they insisted on helping to "change" him so he could meet his maker in Heaven one day.

Quinn's mom followed his gaze.

"That motherfucker," she muttered.

"*Mom.*" Quinn's eyes widened. He'd never heard her use that kind of language. She and Dad had defended him plenty over the years, resulting in yelling matches with the family and slammed doors. Never curses.

"Well, I've had it," she said irritably. "You can't like men but he can gamble away his pension and drink himself into a stupor? How Christian of him." She sneered.

Quinn gathered her close and grinned into the kiss he dropped at the side of her head. "You're awesome, Mom."

"Yeah, yeah, and you're gonna miss me." She pinched his side but didn't break the hug. "Seriously, Quinn. How sure are you about this?" She looked up at him. "You and Declan, I mean."

He smiled and brushed away some hair from her forehead. "I can't predict the future, but five thousand miles won't stand in my way of being with him."

She sighed. "Romantic and a smooth talker like your father. All right." With a gentle pat to his cheek, she stepped back. "Let me break it to Daddy, though. He thinks Miami's too far away for his boy to live. Imagine what he'll think about Alaska."

Quinn was about to answer when movement in the corner of his eye drew his attention to the kitchen window again. A black car parked right outside the house, and he wondered if another aunt or uncle had bought a new vehicle and wanted to drop off more shit about why Adam and Steve was wrong.

It wasn't, though. A man stepped out of the car wearing jeans, a white T-shirt, and sexy wayfarer shades. Quinn knew that body. He knew that messy hair. He knew that face.

Holy shit.

Evidently, Quinn's mom knew him, too. "Oh! Isn't that…"

Quinn's legs were already moving. His heart wasn't; it was stuck in his throat while his ears rang loudly. Thankfully, his body seemed to react just fine. Ripping the door open in the hallway, he stalked outside.

Declan saw him, his mouth stretching into a warm smile, and just as Quinn flew into him, he circled his arms around Quinn.

"Hi, baby," Declan whispered.

"You're here," Quinn croaked. He tightened his hold, feeling all that solid strength under his touch. "You're actually here." The scent—that familiar fucking scent… It was amazing. "Christ, I've missed you." Declan's scruff rasped against his cheek, and Quinn nuzzled closer where the smell of home was stronger.

"I missed you, too." Declan's thick murmur made Quinn shudder. "Let me look at you." He palmed Quinn's jaw and brushed his thumbs under Quinn's eyes. "Fucking beautiful."

Quinn's fingers dug into Declan's hips, trembling. Hell, his entire being was shaking. It was overwhelming to see Declan, and Quinn needed to get even closer. This wasn't enough.

"Why are you here?" Quinn started planting kisses all over. Declan's cheeks, nose, jaw, neck, mouth. "Wait—" Something occurred to him. "You weren't on your way from Nome when we talked, were you?"

Declan smiled softly and shook his head. "I was in Anchorage trying to get a flight." He pressed a kiss between Quinn's brows. "And to answer your first question, I'm here because of three things." While Quinn couldn't seem to stop kissing every inch of

Declan's face, Declan brought out his phone, tapped on the screen a few times, and held it up. *Oh, shit.* It was Quinn's tacky love declaration. "I have to respond to this, of course." He grinned and stole a quick smooch. "I love you too, Quinn. More than I can describe."

It felt like someone squeezed the air out of Quinn's lungs, but it was strangely euphoric. Light-headed, happier than ever, and...well, slightly turned on, he leaned close and pressed his nose to the crook of Declan's neck.

Declan chuckled under his breath. "You know I can feel you, right?"

"Shut up. It's your fault I get hard," Quinn mumbled. "Maybe you should punish me or something."

A low growl rumbled from Declan's chest, and he whispered "Don't tempt me, sweet boy" in Quinn's ear before getting back on track. "I want to show you this next." His phone came up again, and Quinn forced his gaze to follow. "What do you think?"

Quinn frowned, not sure what he was looking at. It was a photo of...a living room? An empty room. Dark hardwood floors, white walls—bare. It appeared to open up to another area too, perhaps a kitchen. There was a long bar where stools would go. That was it. There were also sliding doors that opened up to a balcony. Squinting at the half-grainy picture, he thought he could see the outline of mountains.

Then Declan flipped to another photo. Empty, again. Bedroom? Carpeted floor, same white walls. And then the next photo. A bathroom. Simple, modern, tiled. And more photos. Hallway, a second room—or bedroom—open kitchen that was linked to the living room.

Quinn remained confused, but a tingling sensation crept up his spine. This meant something. These photos were significant, he knew. Gut feeling.

"What is this?" he asked quietly.

"A condo in Anchorage." Declan kept scanning through the photos. "I thought nothing could beat living at the Retreat. Then this amazing guy left, and the place was suddenly hell on earth." He lifted his gaze from the phone to look Quinn in the eye. "I love my brother's place, but since you came back into my life, I can't enjoy the Retreat unless you're there with me."

"You can," Quinn blurted out, his heart pounding. He rambled quickly for fear he wouldn't get all words out. "I told my mom today I'm moving. Logan knows, too. I wanna be with you, and that cabin is home to me now—"

Looking shocked, Declan still managed cut him off. "Take a breath, baby." He cupped the back of Quinn's neck and tucked away his phone. "While it's...*indescribable*...to hear that, you deserve more than Population Zero."

"I was gonna suggest we travel sometimes." Quinn threw that in there.

Declan laughed softly and kissed him on the forehead. "You're a sweetheart. But I see your 'travel sometimes' and raise you one home in Anchorage. When I came here today, my suggestion was that I go back and forth every now and then to be there for Pat and Nina—and that I get a second job in the city."

"That's crazy, Declan." Quinn shook his head. "It's not a quick trip to the grocery store we're talking here. It's a long ride in a death machine."

"We can be flexible, then," Declan said with a smile. "The summer is beautiful up there. Nineteen hours a day of your precious sunshine—well, daylight at least—and..." He released a breath and gently knocked their foreheads together. "What I'm saying is we can split our time. Live in both places. I have to be there during the dead months and the summer because that's when we expand, but there's spring and fall, too. We could be in Anchorage then."

It was getting difficult to argue. Quinn wasn't even sure why he kept doing it. "You don't like Anchorage."

"I wasn't fair there." Declan cringed slightly. "When you brought up Anchorage, I didn't take the hint. I didn't know you were feeling me out. What I told you is true—in my opinion—but there was one thing I didn't see coming."

"What's that?" Quinn's heart drummed faster. Everything he wanted was within reach now.

"I spent a couple days there with Pat," Declan revealed. "I

wanted to find a place, and I only had you in mind. I kept thinking about what you would like, where you'd like to eat, where we'd buy food, which neighborhood would suit you best. And somewhere along the road, I started picturing our life there. I saw us going to a bar to have a couple beers with John and Alex. I saw us taking Kiery along the hiking trails outside town. I pictured us as any other couple heading out to buy groceries and cooking together… The city life suddenly held a big appeal to me, too—"

Quinn was sold. He smashed his mouth to Declan's and kissed him hard.

"I love you," he mumbled into the kiss. "I want that—I wanna live there with you." He parted his lips and met the soft, wet tip of Declan's tongue with his own. "Although, I'm surprised you didn't mention Lola."

Declan smirked and deepened the kiss. "She's too integrated with the pack and would go nuts living indoors all hours of the day. Kiery can be our city pup."

They kissed for several minutes, breaking away only to repeat how much they'd missed each other and to say how relieved they were. Declan, especially. Quinn was thrilled to the point where he ended up chuckling the last time Declan thanked Quinn for wanting to move.

"Oh, I almost forgot." Declan licked his lips, breathing heavily, and retrieved something from his back pocket. "It's nothing much yet, but it's a start. I'll add a gift card whenever I can."

Quinn opened the wrinkled paper folder to see vouchers from an airline.

Declan ran a hand through his hair and explained. "Whenever you wanna see your family, we can go. Or if you wanna go on your own—your call. I want you to have the option."

"When I thought I couldn't love you more…" Quinn shook his head slowly, in awe of the man in front of him. "But we'll save together. We save together, we vacation together. That's the deal."

"Fair enough." Declan stroked Quinn's cheek briefly, then looked around him a little. "Okay, not to freak you out, but we have an audience."

Quinn looked up then too, and he saw a handful of family members on the front lawns of their homes along the street. One look over his shoulder told him his parents, Logan, and Justin were here, as well.

"Forget about freaking *me* out," Quinn said as he saw Aunt Lynn three houses away and across the street. From what he could tell, she didn't appear happy. "Wanna wave to your ex?"

Declan shot him a look at that.

Quinn didn't care one *fucking* bit. He knew now that he had done nothing wrong whatsoever to deserve Aunt Lynn's treatment, so he no longer had to play nice.

"Do you mind if I kick her in the crotch?" Quinn asked, hopeful. "Figuratively speaking, of course."

Declan narrowed his eyes. "You're hardly the kind of man to make a spectacle."

No, Quinn usually wasn't. Now, he was on the top of the world. He had a future to look forward to with the man he loved, and it was about time to wish his family—not counting his parents—a sincere fuck you.

Quinn had always been smart enough to know his preaching family members were simply too stupid to get with the program. So aside from humor, it had only ever been pity he'd felt when they got started with their bullshit. But having a little fun at their expense wasn't wrong, was it?

"Hey, Aunt Lynn!" Quinn called, cupping his mouth. "Did you get some work done or do you always look bitter these days?"

Lynn dropped her jaw before rage took over. "How *dare* you, Quinn! Hank! Are you gonna let him speak to me like that?"

"Oh, dear. I can't watch this," Mom muttered, then headed in inside with Justin.

"I'll give you a full report, love," Dad said. He addressed Lynn next. "Miami's turned Quinn into a real savage, sis. I'm afraid there's nothin' I can do." With amusement lighting up his eyes, he waved a hand at Quinn. "Carry on, son."

"Don't worry, Lynn." Quinn smirked. He linked his fingers with Declan's. "I can keep him happy." That said, he turned to the rest of the family members. A handful was now a dozen. "Y'all remember Declan, right? Now if you'll excuse us, we're gonna go sodomize the fuck out of each other. You can go learn about the earth not being flat."

"Don't do this, son!" Uncle George hollered from two houses over. "We love you, and we won't give up on you!"

"Blah," Quinn said, making a face. "It's like talking to a brick wall. Come on, let's go inside."

"I am so fucking glad we're gonna live thousands of miles away from here." Declan sighed and smiled ruefully. "I'm torn. Part of me is proud and the other wants to turn your ass red."

Quinn waggled his brows.

When they got inside the house, everyone was waiting for them in the kitchen.

"It's good to see you again, Declan," Dad said and extended his hand.

Declan shook it firmly and nodded. "You too, Hank."

Quinn spied his mom scowling at the salad she was making, so he made his way over. "Are you mad, Mom?"

She scoffed. "No."

"But…?" he prodded gently.

She glared at him before using her knife on the tomatoes with more force than was necessary. "No buts. You deserved to tell them where they can shove it. It's just that I have to see them for church on Sunday."

"I'm sorry." He kissed the side of her head. "It felt good, though. You should try it." He winked at her.

That coaxed a smile out of her. "I just might. We'll see."

"Hey, Quinn?" Logan asked. "Can I talk to you for a sec?"

Quinn nodded and passed Declan with a quick kiss. Then he followed Logan and Justin to the living room.

"What's up?"

Justin reached for Quinn, who picked him up and positioned him on his hip.

"I need a favor," Logan admitted. He looked a little nervous. "It's good to see you with Declan, and what you did out there was fucking awesome. So…how about we *don't* ruin the day by telling Declan I tried to kiss you?"

Quinn pretended to be shocked, and he turned to Justin. "I think Daddy's asking me to lie for him." Chuckling, he faced Logan again and draped an arm around his shoulders. "How about this," he said, 'cause he didn't want to hide anything from Declan, "when I tell him, we'll be in Alaska, and he'll have time to cool down his possessive ass before you come visit."

"Your suggestion sucks," Logan told him frankly.

Quinn rolled his eyes. "Honestly, I don't think he'll get mad at all. For one, you didn't actually manage to kiss me." Not where it counted, anyway. "For two, circumstances give you a pass. Declan knows what you're going through. He'll understand and hopefully give me a rough round in the bedroom to make sure I know I'm his."

"TMI, dude." Logan made a face and grabbed Justin.

Quinn shrugged.

"So, when're you leavin'?" Logan asked.

Quinn had no idea. He was ready to get on a plane yesterday, but moving across the country took more planning than that. He looked forward to quitting his job and starting a search for a new one in Alaska, and then there was his family here to say goodbye to and stuff that needed to be shipped.

"I doubt Declan will stay longer than the weekend," he said pensively. "He has a job to return to. So if all goes well, I'll follow him in a couple weeks or so." He studied Logan for any signs of dismay or worry, but there were none. "You okay with this?"

Logan smirked. "I'm fine, Quinn. I'm sorry for freaking out yesterday. It was one of those days. I'm happy for you. And maybe hell will freeze over so I can visit you up there."

"It's the most beautiful place I've ever seen." Quinn would make sure Logan saw it. Soon. "You get used to the cold."

Logan was smiling politely at something behind Quinn, so he turned and saw Declan and Dad approaching. Declan was humoring him with fishing stories, though they stopped when they reached Quinn and Logan.

"You haven't said much, Dad," Quinn noted. After all, it was fairly obvious to anyone now that he was moving, and Mom had requested to bring it up to Dad alone.

Dad smiled wryly. "About what? You movin' to Alaska, or Declan keepin' it in the family?"

Declan winced. "That's an image I could've lived without, Hank."

Dad laughed gruffly. "It's okay, kiddo." He ruffled Quinn's hair. "Of course I wish you'd live here in Sarasota, but I guess you can't really beat the fishin' up in Alaska."

Yeah...*that* was why Quinn was moving. Because of the fishing.

EPILOGUE

One year later...

Anchorage was beautiful in May, though it wasn't the mountains or the pink- and orange-splashed sky outside the window that stole Declan's breath this morning. It was the man writhing underneath him.

"Why do you always have to tease me?" Quinn groaned into his pillow.

"Because it's fun." Declan was straddling the backs of Quinn's thighs, hands spreading his perfect ass cheeks, and watching as the head of his cock disappeared into Quinn.

In this position, Declan was pretty much pushing Quinn down into the mattress, and he couldn't let go of those cheeks. He kneaded them firmly as he inched in and out of that tight hole, slick with lube.

"You always get so desperate when I tease you," Declan murmured. "Desperate enough to wake me up prepared." That was exactly what had happened. Quinn had woken him up with wet kisses and a few greedy sucks on his cock. Then he'd presented his ass for Declan, already lubed up. If that wasn't desperate and goddamn glorious, Declan didn't know what was.

Pulling out, Declan slid his cock along Quinn's crack. Then he teased a bit more by rubbing the tip across the opening, watching as pre-come seeped out.

"But," Quinn panted, "we don't have a lot of time, remember? Oh my God, please fuck me."

Begging did it. Declan pushed forward, and this time he didn't stop until he was buried all the way in. They both moaned, and Declan drew them back so Quinn was up on all fours. That way, Declan could get his hands on Quinn's cock.

"Oh, fuck…" Quinn hung his head and met every thrust, moaning and quivering. "More—oh, fuck, fuck!" His hands fisted the sheets tightly. "Holy shit, I love you."

Declan let out a strained laugh, breathy and husky. "Good thing you've agreed to marry me, then."

After a dark winter full of work around the Retreat, Declan had bought them a trip to Key West where he'd popped the question to Quinn. He'd also arranged for Pam and Hank to come down for a celebratory dinner.

Quinn chuckled, though it morphed into a moan as Declan withdrew then slid in again. "You beat me to it by a damn week."

Further proof they were perfect for each other. Quinn had apparently planned on proposing the week Declan showed him where he grew up in Kodiak. But the trip to Key West had taken place before.

"I love you." Declan leaned over Quinn and kissed his neck. He could feel Quinn was getting close, his cock throbbing in Declan's hand. "Don't make a mess on the sheets." They were leaving first thing in the morning, after all. "Wanna fuck my ass or my mouth, sweet boy?"

Quinn shuddered. "*Please.* Your mouth—*fuck.*"

"Okay. Hold on." He let go of Quinn's cock and chased his own orgasm. As he drove into Quinn's tight ass from behind, Declan felt the muscles in his back rippling with each thrust. "Let me just feed this gorgeous ass my come."

"Give it to me," Quinn groaned. "I need it."

Declan growled, beyond turned on, and quickened his movements. He felt feverish and ready to explode. "Squeeze my cock, Quinn."

Quinn obeyed and clenched his already tight muscles around Declan's erection.

Seconds later, Declan surrendered to his climax and emptied himself inside Quinn.

Fuck, Declan was spent. He fell forward and tried to catch his breath, but with a needy fiancé beneath him, his priorities changed. Screw breathing. He pulled out his softening cock and then rolled Quinn over and settled between his thighs.

Quinn pushed himself up on his elbows and stared through hooded eyes as Declan sucked him in. For one beat, Quinn threw his head back in pleasure and moaned.

Declan hummed around the warm, heavy cock, loving the taste. Their gazes locked when he swirled his tongue around the come-coated head.

"Fingers," Quinn gasped. "Please—need 'em."

Declan was happy to oblige, and it didn't take long for him to find Quinn's prostate. He stroked it gently with two fingers and tightened his lips to suck Quinn harder.

A groan escaped Declan. The smell of morning sex, the feeling of Quinn's soaked ass around his fingers, and the flavor of his cock on Declan's tongue were enough to cause his own cock to want more.

There'd be time for that tonight or tomorrow when they got to the Retreat.

"Now," Quinn choked out. After that, his body went rigid, and Declan swallowed his release greedily. "Oh, my fuck…"

Declan wished they could spend all day in bed, but they had a lot to do. As Quinn melted into the mattress and panted heavily, Declan kissed his way up Quinn's body until their mouths met.

"Shower with me?" Declan murmured.

Quinn hummed and nibbled at Declan's bottom lip. "Hell, yeah."

*

When the doorbell rang, Declan left the kitchen—Kiery following happily—wiped his hands on a dish towel, and headed to the hallway.

Opening the door, he saw three familiar faces that had become a permanent fixture for every winter at the Retreat.

"Hey, man!" Alex was quick to hand over a bottle of a nice whiskey. "The missus says hi."

"Damn, you didn't have to bring anything. Come on in, guys." Declan opened the door wider to let John, Alex, and Kyle inside. Now that Declan and Quinn spent almost half their time in Anchorage, they saw the cousins often enough. Declan even worked with John in construction every now and then, and they had dinner together sometimes. But they almost only saw Kyle for expansions at the Retreat.

"Where's Wolf?" Declan asked, referring to Kiery's brother. The two pups—though they were fully grown now—were away from the Retreat too much to be a part of the pack, so Wolf and Kiery stayed together whenever they saw each other.

"Barrow. My dad wanted to borrow him for a hunt," Kyle replied. "I'll bring him next time." He bent down to pet Kiery. "So where's the ball-and-chain-to-be?"

"Picking up his buddy at the airport," Declan replied. "Here, let me take your bag. Did you just get in?"

Kyle nodded. "Mitch's son had business up in Barrow, so I flew down with him."

A lot of going back and forth for him, then. From tomorrow on, they'd enjoy a week at Retreat, for the first time as guests. Declan and Quinn had their cabin as always, and Pat and Nina were putting the others in cabins this time, too. It was an engagement gift. One week, Declan and Quinn with their closest.

"Well, let's get a drink." Declan appraised the whiskey bottle with a smile. "Dinner's almost ready, and Quinn and Logan can catch up when they get here."

Logan would probably need it. Declan hadn't seen him since last year, but they said hello in passing whenever Quinn and Logan Skyped. No lie, Declan had been ticked off when he'd learned about the kiss, though it had been fairly easy to let go of. Logan was doing better, even while he still had a lot on his plate. The guy needed this vacation.

Unlike Quinn, Logan had no fears about flying. He'd need a drink for another reason. It was the first time he would be away from his kid, who was gonna stay with Pam and Hank for the week.

Quinn's folks had been invited, but since they'd celebrated with them in Key West, they thought this was the perfect time to take Justin to Disney World.

"Wow. Check this out, all homey and cozy." Kyle smirked as he eyed the living room. Last time he'd been here, the condo had still been pretty bare.

Little by little, Declan and Quinn had created their second home with ease. Furniture, either built by Declan or bought. Books, movies, photos on the walls… John's wife had dropped by one day with drapes, rugs, and decorative pillows and blankets. She said it was necessary.

John chuckled and poked the single plant on the coffee table. "I'm surprised this one's still alive."

"It's been touch and go a few times," Declan admitted. It wouldn't make it this summer. After their vacation, Declan and Quinn were staying until September. Lots of work to do, and Quinn would alternate between being a handyman and working on his new online marketing business. He'd already worked wonders with the Retreat's website.

Checking the salmon, Declan asked if they'd settled on where Kyle was staying tonight. He was welcome here, but Logan would spend the night here, as well. Then again, there was space for them both—a spare bed in the guest room and a pullout couch in the living room.

"I'll stay here if you don't mind," Kyle said. "The only kid I can handle is my niece."

"*Painfully* true." Alex snickered as he got three glasses out of a cabinet. "Last time he slept in our guest room, he almost had a panic attack when my boys wanted to play Go Fish with him."

"Hey, I don't fucking know the protocol," Kyle defended, grabbing a Coke instead of whiskey. "Do I let them win, do I beat them and teach them they can't always win, would they cry—fuck me, I'd shoot myself if they cried. It was too much." He shook his head, seemingly intent to ignore the other three laughing at him. "John, your kids are worse. Preteens." He shuddered.

Declan chuckled and removed the potatoes from the stove, pouring out the water so he could mash 'em. "Well, no kids here this time." Quinn's ultimate goal was for Logan to move here too, and he knew Justin was the key. If Quinn could make a child fall for the state, perhaps Logan would follow.

"Where do you keep the plates?" Alex asked, sliding a glass of whiskey to Declan.

"Right here." Declan opened a cabinet before taking a sip of his drink. "I'll go get the other stools." There were only four of them around the kitchen bar now, so he went to the closet in the hallway and took out two more.

The men were almost done with their first drink when Kiery barked and rushed toward the door. Two seconds later, keys wriggled in the door, and Quinn and Logan arrived.

"There's my girl," Declan heard Quinn greet Kiery. "Did'ju miss Daddy? Yeah, you did."

"It's the ball and chain!" Kyle held up his glass.

Declan smiled as Quinn emerged, shrugging off his hoodie.

"I can be the chain. Someone else can be the ball," Quinn said. "Damn, somethin' smells great in here." He made a beeline for Declan and gave him a kiss before he started greeting their friends. And once that was done, Logan appeared from the hallway, too. "So, Logan. That's John and Alex—they're cousins, live here in town, and work with us up at the Retreat sometimes. And that's Kyle; he lives way up north, is the proud owner of Kiery's brother, and if he's not out hunting big game, he's an electrician. Everyone, this is Logan. Fellow Floridian who overpacked and brought seven scarves and beanies."

"Obviously. It's cold as fuck here," Logan muttered. He ripped off his hat and shuddered. "This is supposed to be *May*?"

"You get used to it," Quinn laughed. "And this isn't all that cold. It's nice out."

Declan was amused. He wouldn't have been able to *pay* Quinn to say that a year ago.

"I'm revoking your Florida citizenship," Logan said, shaking his head. Then he smiled politely and faced the others. "Nice to meet y'all. Quinn's told me a lot about you guys."

"We're worse than that." Alex smirked. "Whiskey?"

*

After dinner, jokes, and beers, the men decided they'd go to a bar. Declan and Quinn had become regulars at a British pub in their neighborhood, so it was the obvious choice. Opening the door, Declan let Quinn enter first, and the rest followed.

Drinks and snacks were ordered, and they found a booth big enough to seat everyone.

"I'm glad we're all gathered," Quinn said for only Declan to hear.

Declan nodded and placed his arm along the back of the booth behind Quinn. "Definitely. More witnesses to see Tipsy Quinn appear." He winked and bussed Quinn's cheek.

"Where's the bathroom?" Logan asked.

John answered while Quinn told Declan he was a subtle drunk. And wasn't that the lie of the year?

"If you say so, baby," Declan laughed.

"What're you lovebirds whispering about?" Alex grinned.

"Declan implies I'm a wild drunk," Quinn said with a snort.

Declan pursed his lips. "I wouldn't say wild. Just adorable and funny as fuck. Flushed cheeks, glazed-over eyes, and you tend to *giggle*."

"Oh, yeah! I remember that," Alex laughed.

"That's even worse, though," Kyle said, sliding out of the booth. "Drunk and sporting a hard-on for Declan, he *still* beat us in swimming." Quinn thought that was funny, and he nodded in agreement. Kyle chuckled. "I'll be back—gotta take a leak."

He disappeared, and Declan turned to see Quinn smirking at him.

"You didn't beat *me*," Declan reminded him.

That brought out a scowl from his fiancé. "You cheated!"

"Not that again," John groaned through a laugh. "When we get up there tomorrow, we should just do a rematch."

Declan and Quinn argued back and forth on how Declan had won their race, but in the end, John's suggestion was best. They'd have to do it again, and Declan would simply come up with a new way to win.

"Count me in." Quinn took a swig from his beer and lifted a brow at Declan. "Think you can handle the heat, sweetheart?"

Oh, the kid was going *down*. "You bet."

"I hear 'bet' and I come running." Kyle had returned, and he slid into his seat again and reached for a bottle of water. "What're we betting on?"

"Rematch in swimming," Alex answered, grinning.

"Oh, I'm in too," Kyle said seriously.

Logan reappeared again as well, and Declan wasn't sure if it was the dim lighting in the pub, but it looked like Logan was flustered. Quinn didn't notice though, so maybe it was in Declan's head.

"Okay, a toast." John raised his beer. "To Declan and Quinn, congrats on your engagement, and to a great time on our vacation."

Declan and Quinn exchanged a wide smile and a quick kiss as the others echoed the toast.

"All right, let's get hammered, boys!" Alex divided shots from a tray in the middle of the table. "If we're lucky, Quinn will sleep the entire way so we don't have to hear him saying we're gonna die."

Quinn flipped him off but laughed. "Don't get me too drunk, unless you wanna carry me to the airport tomorrow morning."

Alex only pointed to Declan. "That's his job now, buddy."

"For better or for worse." Declan shrugged and smiled. "He moved across the entire country for me. I think I can exchange a threshold on our wedding day for a terminal at the airport."

The guys cracked up, and Quinn grabbed Declan's jaw and said, "Isn't he the sweetest?" He smacked a loud smooch to Declan's lips. And then he moved close to Declan's ear. "I love you to stupidity, but we can't have you thinkin' it's all you." Declan smiled down between them, knowing what was next. Quinn had said it before. "I came for the man and stayed for both him and the north."

That was exactly how Declan wanted it.

Love could take you thousands of miles, but why make the journey if you didn't enjoy the destination?

QUINN AND DECLAN RETURN IN NORTHLAND, LOGAN AND KYLE'S STORY, WHICH IS NOW AVAILABLE FOR PURCHASE.

*

Excerpt 1

"No, it's okay. I've got this," Quinn assured Logan. "Justin and I are gonna be best friends this winter. Ain't that right, buddy?"

"Yeah," Justin laughed and munched on a fry.

Logan tried to relax. What Quinn had said was true. He'd turned out to be a decent handyman—which Logan was only a little surprised about—but a lot of the work this year required more than that. So Quinn would take on lighter tasks while watching Justin.

"Eat. Unclench," Quinn told Logan pointedly. Then he looked at something behind Logan, and it turned out to be Declan. "You don't look happy."

"No." Declan sat down and sighed heavily. "One of our orders won't go through in Anchorage, and I can't fly down to check it out. I have three more shipments to approve here, and Pat can't leave the Retreat."

"What kind of shipment is it?" Logan asked.

Declan picked up his burger, though he didn't appear very hungry. "Heaters and timber."

NORTHBOUND

"I can do it," Logan offered with a shrug. Quinn was one of the few people he was comfortable enough to leave Justin with, and it sounded like a quick trip. He could fly there now, then be on the first flight back to Nome tomorrow morning. "Unless you wanna send Valium boy over there." He jerked his chin at Quinn.

"My middle finger. Picture it," Quinn said flatly. "And when're people gonna learn it's only the bush planes I don't like? Y'all don't see me bitching when we go from Nome to Anchorage. So excuse me if I indulge in the barest amount of magical medication when we fly with Mitch."

"Easy, baby," Declan chuckled. "You're in luck. Mitch's son is flying us up later, and his plane is bigger. Otherwise we wouldn't fit the cargo." Next, he slid his gaze to Logan. "I'd really appreciate if you could go with Kyle."

Hold the fuck up. "Kyle?" It suddenly felt like Logan had a noose around his neck.

*

Excerpt 2

"Come on, over there." Kyle ushered Lani toward Declan's table, and they saw him when they were a dozen feet away.

"Look who it is!" Quinn was…carefree and happy.

Kyle grinned faintly and quirked a brow at Declan. "He on Valium already?"

"For the love of…" Quinn grumbled.

"No, but he made his coffee Irish," Declan said with a smirk. "Good to see you, Kyle. This is your niece, I assume?"

"Yeah…" Kyle placed a hand on her head. "Lani here sorta held me at gunpoint." That made Lani giggle and the rest chuckle. "Anyway, I know we're off to Anchorage, but she won't get in the way and I'll buy an extra ticket for her."

Declan waved that off. "Don't worry about it. You remember Logan, right? You'll be going with him instead." He went on to explain the situation and why Declan couldn't tag along, and Kyle nodded and shook Logan's hand.

Not much had changed with Logan Ward. He was still hot as fuck, all hard edges and warm colors. Kyle couldn't decide if he liked the trimmed beard or the brown eyes more, but it didn't matter.

When they'd first met, they'd all gone out to a pub after dinner at Declan and Quinn's place, and Kyle and Logan had ended up going to the bathroom at the same time. There, Kyle had casually asked if Logan was looking forward to the vacation up at the Retreat, and Logan's response had been to grunt something unintelligible and stumble into a stall.

During their vacation, whenever Kyle said anything, Logan had only offered clipped answers and hasty getaways.

Whatever Logan had against him wasn't Kyle's problem.

"Declan and I are leaving as soon as the shipments have been cleared," Quinn said. "We're bringing Justin with us, and Lani is welcome to join us, too. And Wolf—you've brought him, right?"

"He's outside," Kyle answered with a nod. He looked down at Lani. "It's up to you, *miki*. Either you come with me to the city, or you go to the Retreat."

"Can I go fishing?" Lani asked hopefully.

"No," Kyle replied with a quiet laugh. "None of that until I get there."

She pursed her lips, thinking it over.

"I think we're just gonna settle in and maybe spend some time with the dogs." Quinn smiled at her. "There are new puppies if that matters."

"Oh, that matters," Lani said. "I'd definitely like to join you, please. Thank you for offering."

She could be polite to others, eh?

"She's a cutie." Quinn grinned at Kyle.

"You say that because you're not her uncle," Kyle replied dryly.

"Okay, so it's settled." Declan pulled out a set of keys. "You can stay at our place, of course. I'll head over to the airport with you. Hopefully, our food is there now, and I gotta get you tickets, too."

"You sure about this?" Logan asked Quinn, appearing

nervous.

Could be one of two reasons, Kyle reckoned. One, he was uncomfortable leaving his kid. Two, he didn't wanna travel with Kyle.

Kyle had no fucks to give, so he went to the register to order some food to go.

FOR MORE, VISIT
www.caradeewrites.com
CARA ON SOCIAL MEDIA

- FACEBOOK.COM/CARADEEWRITES
- @CARADEEWRITES
- @CARAWRITES